The Oxley Crossing Romances

Australian Rural Romance

Electing Robert Whitman

LENA WEST

Gymea Publishing

Published by Gymea Publishing

https://www.facebook.com/LenaWestAuthor/

www.lenawestauthor.com

ISBN-13: 978-0-6482671-0-2

Disclaimer

This story is a work of fiction.

Names, characters, places and incidents are the product of the author's imagination and are used fictitiously. Any resemblance to events, locales or actual persons, living or dead, is entirely coincidental.

Some actual locations may be referenced in passing.

Table of Contents

ELECTING ROBERT WHITMAN

Dedication

This novel is dedicated to Adam and Wendy. Your encouragement means so much to me.

ELECTING ROBERT WHITMAN

1

Something good was about to happen.

She could 'feel it in her water' as Gran used to say. Maybe she'd meet the man she was destined to fall in love with. She was at a wedding, after all, with romance casting its aura far and wide, so that was not an unreasonable assumption.

Anticipation humming through her veins lent added sparkle to Sophie James's warm, brown eyes as, stopping frequently to exchange greetings, she strolled between the tables in the main auditorium of the Oxley Crossing Bowling Club, searching for the place card bearing her name. She had expected to be on the same table as her mother, whose invited partner she was at this wedding, but while her mother was happily seated at a table of older people, several of whom were ranked among her particular cronies, she herself was still looking for her place.

She was lucky to be able to attend, as she wasn't often in The Crossing, now she was working full time in Port Macquarie.

When her mother had asked her to be the 'and partner' on her invitation, she had jumped at the chance of a night out with the old crowd. That alone was reason enough for her upbeat mood, but she was certain the tingle in her blood was a premonition of something far more important than a simple night out with friends. If that was all it took to get her feeling like this, she'd be tingling madly every other time she poked her nose out the door.

Even though she didn't know either Geni Sullivan or Ben Wright particularly well, she liked them both and was happy to be celebrating with them tonight. Theirs had been a dramatic, whirlwind romance which almost came to grief when Geni's violent ex-husband had kidnapped her. That event, with its tragic outcome for Nigel Blount, Geni's ex, had been the talk of The Crossing ever since, although the recent birth of the Armitage baby had almost toppled it from top spot.

"Hey Sophie," she looked up as Joey Lambert whistled and called out to attract her attention. "You're over here with us. Looks like this table was reserved for young singles."

Well, that makes sense, Sophie thought.

Smiling, she made her way to join Joey and the handful of other young people, all of whom she had gone to school with several years earlier. Good friends all of them. Some better than others, she thought, spotting her one-time BFF, Pam Lanner approaching. Knowing everyone was one of the advantages of growing up in a small town. It was also one of the disadvantages; since there was always someone who knew where the dirt was buried. There were no secrets in a small town, something newcomers often failed to realise until too late.

Being a total stranger in the regional city of Port Macquarie, she was still somewhat ambivalent about the anonymity of her position there. Not that she'd have to be concerned about it for much longer.

Her plum job had been as a temporary replacement for a woman on extended maternity leave, who now wanted her job back. Not unexpected, but Sophie had been hoping the new mum would be so enamoured with motherhood she'd choose to stay away a while longer. Long enough for *her* to really impress the boss with her valuable contribution to the company, and maybe be offered a permanent position of her own.

Sophie had told her mother over breakfast. She wasn't looking forward to joining the multitude of aspiring hopefuls all with their ambitions pinned on the rare vacancies in the most prestigious companies, but Dorothy, her mother, had had serious news of her own. Only half attending to the chatter all around her, Sophie ran the breakfast conversation through her mind once again.

"Sophie dear," her mother had begun, "I have to go into hospital for a little op. My old trouble," she had waved off Sophie's instinctive exclamations. "The difference is, this time the doctors say I need the op or it will just get worse, and then I might be in real trouble."

"I'll take time off to be there at the hospital with you, Mum,"

Sophie reached out to clasp her mother's hand, offering tacit comfort.

"Off course you will, Dear," her mother said.

"It's just, hearing your news, I had the idea you might be able to help me out with another small problem, since you'll be out of work for a little bit right at the time I need someone. It seemed providential, but don't think you have to agree if something comes up for you in the meantime. I know how important your career is to you," her mother had finished up, half apologetically.

Not as important as all that, Sophie thought. She'd be happy to consider a change in direction in her career; if the right opportunity presented itself.

A couple more questions had elicited the whole story. Her mother's full-time assistant in her shop, the Oxley Crossing Newsagent, an experienced woman more than capable of taking over in an emergency, was on holiday. She had taken three months leave and gone to visit family in England. The other assistants, all part-timers, were willing workers, but none of them able to run the business.

"You'd like me to step up and hold the fort till you're back on your feet," Sophie had broken in, cutting off her mother's guilty rambling explanation. "In that case, it really is providential, my being free just when you need me. I'll defer looking for a new job until you're able to take over again."

It wasn't what Sophie had been planning for her immediate future, but her mother had always been there for her, and now the boot was on the other foot, she was happy to fill in. The relief on her mother's face had confirmed the rightness of her snap decision.

Snapping back to her surroundings, Sophie kissed cheeks and exchanged greetings.

She was rather surprised to find herself still dwelling on the subject of her employment. It wasn't as if working in her mother's shop was anything new. She'd spent most of her student holidays working for her mother to supplement her university allowance.

The emcee, Alan Morgan, began shepherding everyone to their tables, as the bridal party was about to make their entrance.

Sophie walked round the table to her spot; and had one of those *déjà vu* moments.

Her table partner was Robert Whitman.

Again.

Just as he had been at the last wedding she'd attended; Megan Patterson's wedding. Sophie laughed silently to herself, willing to bet Eddie Patterson had been responsible both times. Eddie and her propensity for matchmaking were legendary in The Crossing. *Successful matchmaking*, Sophie amended, her heart skipping a beat.

After meeting Robert for the first time in ages, she'd hoped he would follow up on what had been a very enjoyable evening. She supposed it wasn't surprising he hadn't, since they lived in different parts of the country, but she'd felt badly disappointed, nonetheless.

Was this second meeting, an apparent reprise on the last, what was setting off the tingles? Did she want a second chance to attract Robert Whitman's attention?

Then the man himself was there, seating her politely like the gentleman he indisputably was.

His hand rested momentarily on her shoulder, and her pulse kicked into a higher gear.

"Sophie. I didn't know you were home. It's good to see you again."

He actually did sound pleased, Sophie noted. Thus encouraged, she impulsively decided there and then to try her luck with him. At least, she amended, she would make an effort to discover the truth of what she actually felt for the man. Maybe she'd learn all she felt was friendship. And maybe he really was the man for her. Time, and her heart, would tell.

Robert Whitman, whom most people referred to as Bob, wasn't every girl's dream man. *All the better for me*, Sophie concluded, regarding him with a severely critical eye. *Less competition*. The glasses he wore, slightly magnifying his warm hazel eyes, made him appear a bit nerdish.

Intelligent, she corrected herself.

Coupled with his punctilious dress code and a tendency to pontificate when he got on his hobbyhorse, he'd been the butt of unkind jokes at school. But Sophie liked a well-dressed man, and she shared a number of his interests. They'd always had plenty to talk about.

Sophie had always seen below the surface with Robert, and she didn't believe he would have changed fundamentally.

She saw a dark haired, pleasant featured man who was borderline handsome; not particularly tall, but still comfortably taller than herself. Appraising him objectively, she came to the conclusion he would become distinguished looking with the addition of a few more years.

Robert cared passionately about his family and friends, his country and his community. Sentiments with which she agreed wholeheartedly.

I really like Robert Whitman. A lot, she concluded happily.

She always had, ever since the time he'd come to the rescue, when, a timid five-year old, she'd been teased at school. A high school boy at the time, his support had carried weight among her young classmates. After that, he'd made a point of seeing she was okay until it became obvious she'd found her feet; although he'd continued to wave or call a greeting in passing. He always had.

Little Sophie had silently adored her champion from afar. Years later, teenage Sophie had met him on one of his visits home from university, and the adoration had blossomed into her first full-blown crush.

Which I have never entirely outgrown, she realised.

Adult Sophie wondered if a closer relationship might be possible now the once prohibitive age divide between them had narrowed to acceptability.

"It's good to see you, too, Robert," she responded with an almost intimate smile. "I miss my friends so much when I'm away."

There was no time for more until the servers began circulating with the entrees, and even then, conversation was general, with various topics being batted back and forth around the table as everyone caught up on the latest happenings. Sophie bided her time until attention turned mainly to food.

Robert wasn't sure sitting next to little Sophie James was a particularly good idea. He'd always found her way too attractive for comfort. Considering the age gap between them, he'd felt the attraction to be inappropriate, and had hoped, aided by time and distance, it would disappear. It hadn't.

Last year she'd about knocked him for six when they ended up together at Megan's wedding. He'd come perilously close to forgetting she was off-limits. Just as well she'd gone back to Port Macquarie. Out of sight, but unfortunately, not out of mind. Now he had to cope with her seductive presence all over again, and the worst of it was, one glance had been enough for him to know it would be harder to resist her this time.

"Last time we met, Robert, you were telling me you planned to enter the political arena. Is that still your goal?"

"It is, Soph." Politics. Robert clutched at the lifeline he'd been thrown. If he could keep the conversation safely centred on politics and their future careers, he might just make it through the meal without giving himself away.

"I'm working in Arthur Steedman's office. Our Federal Member of Parliament, you know. He's an Independent, which is what I want to be, and he's grooming me to stand at the next State election in just over a year's time. He reckons I'll be ready by then with a good chance of getting in."

"How wonderful! I think you'll be an excellent rep for this electorate." Sophie chuckled, causing a raised eyebrow. "It just occurred to me, I can come knocking on your door, once you've won your seat, to ask for a recommendation for a back-room job. I'm in public relations, and I'd love to work in the House."

Robert preened guiltily. He wasn't accustomed to admiration from attractive young women, but little Sophie James wasn't like the other girls. Sophie looked up to him; which made remembering not to step out of line with her damned difficult. Although, she was not so little now. He cast a surreptitious, yet extremely comprehensive eye over her lithe, stylishly clad figure, confirming what had disconcerted him so much the year before.

Sophie James had grown up very nicely indeed, with glossy, dark brown hair tumbling smoothly over her shoulders and enticing curves in all the right places. He felt his body responding to her presence, and adjusted his position slightly, giving thanks his dignity was preserved by the table cloth.

It was enough to make him wish he wasn't so much older than her. A young woman like Sophie wouldn't look twice at a man his age with so many more attractive options among her own age group. A sweep of the table, noting the several handsome younger men present, was sufficient to depress any pretensions he might have. If that wasn't enough, there was a city full of eligible young blokes down in Port Macquarie. Imagining Sophie in another man's arms gave him a bad few moments. But she was still talking. He tuned back in to her conversation.

"I noticed the new look, Robert. I like it. Out here in the bush, the designer stubble makes you stand out in a crowd. Was it your girlfriend's idea?"

The last bit was shamelessly added so she could determine his current status without giving herself away by asking the question outright.

"Thanks. I think. It was accidental really. I was running late one morning and didn't have time to shave. Mrs Steedman approved of the new look and suggested I cultivate it."

He remembered Sophie's tail-end question, debating whether or not to ignore it. He shrugged mentally. If she didn't hear it from him, someone else would probably fill her in, and really, it didn't matter, did it?

"No girlfriend. I seem to be plagued with the worst luck when it comes to romance." He grimaced. "Mum tells me to stop worrying about it. She reckons I'll know the right woman when I see her, then everything will be smelling of roses."

"She's undoubtedly right." Sophie placidly reverted to discussing his political career, but inside she gave a mental air pump. Robert Whitman was still single and available. If that wasn't providence giving her a nudge, she didn't know what was. She didn't know whether her attraction to him would grow into love, but it was stronger than anything she'd felt for the handful of boyfriends she'd had in the past; relationships which had all fizzled out to nothing.

There and then Sophie decided to make the most of her heaven-sent return to The Crossing and explore the possibilities.

"You know, Robert," she leaned closer, her breast 'accidently' brushing against his arm, so he could hear her above the rising noise level, "I'm going to be home for a bit. Mum has to go into hospital in a fortnight, and I'm helping her out in the shop for a few weeks. I'll have plenty of time on my hands, so how would you like it if I helped you get your campaign off the ground?"

Robert's attention had been distracted by the warm weight of her breast pressed against his arm, and her breath caressing his ear, sending an intoxicating shiver down his spine.

He looked startled by Sophie's suggestion. Noticing, she jumped in quickly before he could refuse her help.

"I told you I'd like a job in the House. Working on your campaign would look good on my CV, so how about it?"

~~~~~

Before they left the table, Sophie had wrung a firm agreement from Robert. As soon as she returned to The Crossing in two weeks, she would be working with him in the evenings to plan the most effective political campaign the region had ever seen. The work would be satisfying, career wise, and as for romance… Surely propinquity would reveal her true feelings, and Robert's, one way or the other.

Although, if the sparks they'd kindled during the one dance she'd managed to snaffle with him were any indication, their prospects were promising. As long as the fireworks had been mutual; which, considering he had made no effort to monopolise her during the remainder of the evening, she had yet to determine.

2

Dorothy James had come through her operation with flying colours and was making excellent progress. So much so, her surgeon was returning her to the Oxley Crossing hospital in the morning to complete her recovery under Doc Roberts's care. Sophie checked out of her motel and after one last, quick visit with her mother, hit the road for The Crossing. Now her concern for her mother was allayed, her mind turned to her secret campaign of the heart.

I sound like a soppy romance novel. She grinned at the thought, then began singing along to the radio, happier than she'd been in years, and for a natural optimist, that was saying something.

It was hard to believe how motivated she was to succeed in seeing Robert elected to Parliament. It was the most exciting project she'd had a hand in, and if she did well it would open so many new doors, career-wise. All that, even before she took her romantic aspirations into consideration.

She hadn't wasted any time during her last few days in Port Macquarie.

Researching online, she'd compiled a list of tasks needing to be carried out preparatory to Robert beginning what she had dubbed 'Operation Election.'

He probably thinks I'll be more of a liability than an asset, she thought. *He'll soon learn differently.* Robert Whitman was going to be amazed and astounded at how very, very useful she was going to be in launching his political career.

And, she added thoughtfully to herself, *maybe he'll stop treating me like a kid sister.* She couldn't help wondering if that was the reason he'd repeatedly backed away from her. Last time she'd fancied herself in love with him, her age had been an all too real deterrent to a romantic relationship, but now she was grown up, it was no longer relevant. Or shouldn't be. She reckoned it was up to her to prove that to Robert.

A born list-maker, she started mentally mapping a course of action to solve the problem. With two so very different campaigns to conduct simultaneously, as well as helping in her mother's shop, she was going to be a busy girl in the coming weeks. Sophie laughed out loud, earning a curious look from a woman driving in the opposite direction. Life looked set to become quite exciting.

~~~~~

"Have you heard?"

Hazel Whitman slid her husband's plate in front of him, deliberately ignoring his patent displeasure with its, in his view, meagre contents. Doc Rogers said he needed to lose weight or risk having a heart attack. Since she loved her man, Hazel, following a consultation with the dietician, had placed him on a strict diet, much to his chagrin.

"What are you blathering on about, Woman," Bill muttered irascibly.

"I was on the phone with Eddie just now," Hazel began, ignoring Bill's impatient snort. "Dot James is being sent back here so Doc can take care of her properly and all her friends can pop in to see her."

"I assume that means she's making a good recovery?" This from Robert, their son, who lived in the detached granny flat out the back but ate with them several nights a week.

"Yes, it does, Robert. Eddie says the surgeon is very pleased with her."

"Trust Eddie to have the latest news." Bill knew better than to complain about his diet, but Eddie Patterson with her nose for news, was fair game.

"Oh well. Sophie was in the supermarket this afternoon. She told Carol Tan, who passed it along to Eddie. So it's practically from the horse's mouth."

"I'm sure our Sophie would love to hear you calling her a horse."

Robert, accustomed to his parents' good-natured bickering, sat a little straighter, chewing thoughtfully on his portion of roast lamb. A significantly larger portion than his father's. He swallowed, then waited for a break in the conversation.

"Sophie's back, then?"

"You heard your mother, didn't you Bob? If Sophie was in Tan's this arvo, then it stands to reason, she must be back, doesn't it?"

"Pay no attention to your father, Robert. He's just cranky because Doc put him on a diet. You ought to go round later. See she's alright."

As if Sophie, born and bred in The Crossing wouldn't be all right in her mother's cottage behind the newsagents.

All the same, Robert rather thought he might do as his mother suggested. He'd found himself thinking about Sophie quite often since the wedding. Too often? He wondered. Nothing could come of it, of course. He knew that, but she'd offered to help get his campaign off the ground. Between that and concern for her mother, he had an impeccable excuse to call on her. Although Sophie was just a kid, so while he didn't hold out any great hopes her promise of help would amount to anything useful, it would be nice to see her again.

Maybe if he saw her frequently enough, he'd get over his damned inconvenient infatuation with her and see her as just another nice, ordinary young girl. Nobody special at all.

~~~~~

Robert made his way down the dark lane towards the back of the row of shops. He could see a light on in Dot's cottage, but there were also lights on in the back room of the shop. Mentally flipping a coin, he decided to try the shop first. Why else would the lights be on unless Sophie was in there? Nobody else ought to be.

A brisk tattoo on the back door brought Sophie's head up.

Who's that? She wondered.

The shop closed at five o'clock, so nobody should be hanging about at this time.

Her heart beating a trifle quicker, she began tip-toeing towards the window. This may be good old Oxley Crossing, but no way was she opening the door after dark without getting a good look at her visitor first. Hesitating, she cast a glance over her shoulder at the open safe and detoured to shut it. Seconds later she flung open the door.

"Robert Whitman! You scared the daylights out of me, banging on the door at this hour."

"It's not all that late Sophie. What are you doing out here at night, anyway?"

"Come in Robert." She stepped back and waved him in.

"With both Mum and I in Tamworth, Rose McGowan has been opening the shop the last few days, but she won't touch the paperwork or the banking. It's all dumped in the safe in bags labelled 'Monday', 'Tuesday' etc. I've been doing a bit of catching up on the accounts."

While she talked, she tidied the desk. With Robert on the doorstep it was time to switch roles. The accounts would keep.

"I heard your mum's coming home tomorrow."

She almost asked how he knew but didn't bother. In The Crossing the bush telegraph was quicker, and more reliable, than the internet. With no effort at all she could arrive at a dozen different routes the news might have taken.

"Home to The Crossing," she confirmed, "but she'll be in the hospital a bit longer yet. Would you like a cuppa? I'm ready to pack it in here."

"Sure. I just looked in to see you're okay."

"I'm very much okay, Robert, now I know Mum's going to be fine."

Sophie locked the door and led the way across the delivery bay to the cottage tucked into the back corner of the block. It dated back to the days when most businesses in the town included living quarters for the owners, and, with just the two of them, her mother had never seen a need to move to a larger house.

While Sophie put the kettle on and pottered about with the coffee mugs, Robert stood next to the kitchen doorway, looking about him. It had been a while since he'd been in Dot's house, but nothing much had changed, except for the calendar and the photos held to the door of the fridge with magnets.

They were all of Sophie. Smiling, he edged across for a closer look.

Sophie in mortar board and gown graduating from university. Sophie in sports uniform holding a trophy aloft with a pack of other girls crowding around. Sophie all dressed up for a special occasion. They comprised a photographic record of the highlights in Sophie's life.

Robert let his eyes cruise over the collection, halting with a sinking feeling in the pit of his stomach as his gaze settled on a fairly recent photo in the bottom rank. Sophie on a beach towel, all wrapped up in some young bloke's arms. He recoiled, stepping back too quickly, and bumped into her as she came to put the milk away in the fridge.

"Whoa! Nearly spilt the milk, Rob. Don't want that," she chuckled. "Today's a happy day. No tears allowed. Not even over spilt milk."

"No. You're right. Sorry." Although Robert found it hard to speak past the lump in his throat. That handsome bloke holding Sophie looked prosperous. Successful. Exactly the sort of man to set an impressionable young girl's heart aflutter. Worst of all, he looked young. A suitable age match for Sophie. It felt like the final nail being hammered into the coffin of hopes he refused to acknowledge had ever existed.

"C'mon, Robert. Stop dawdling. I've got a heap of stuff to show you."

Stifling a sigh, Robert followed her through into the family room where Sophie was setting the tray down on the coffee table.

"Help yourself. I'll just get my notes." She hurried off, returning moments later with a bulging loose-leaf folder. As she tossed it down on the table, Robert read the label. **_Electing Robert Whitman._** The certainty of it felt a bit of a backhanded compliment following so closely on the revelation in the kitchen.

"Sit here so you can see, Rob."

Sophie patted the sofa beside her and Robert reluctantly sat where she had indicated. She passed his coffee across to him, and opened the folder, flipping past the introductory pages to the first set of notes which she removed.

"I've been doing a bit of research on electioneering," she said, handing him the sheaf of pages as she continued speaking. "This is a rough list of things we need to do. You probably know all this already, but it's new for me, so I wrote everything down so I wouldn't forget something absolutely vital. Check it over for the things I missed, would you?"

It was Robert's first election too, but he'd helped his father several times in the past when Bill had stood for Shire president, so he did have a fair grasp on the procedures. Difference was, he hadn't put anything in writing, and said so. He turned the pages slowly, reading Sophie's neat, precisely detailed overview.

"This is good, Soph. With a list like this, I can simply tick things off as they get done."

"Exactly what I thought. Here," she passed over another sheaf of pages.

"This is a list of businesses who do the work. You know, printing posters, making TV ads, etc. I sourced as many as I could, with costings, so you can compare. Some sent me samples of their work, but those are in a case I haven't unpacked yet. As you can see, I've put local businesses at the top of the list and marked the ones that look best. I thought it would be good policy to contract locally wherever you can. It might earn you a few extra votes."

Sophie looked up, worry lines creasing her forehead when Robert said nothing.

He wasn't even smiling.

Did he think she'd overstepped the mark? If he did, it would make it awkward for her to help him in the way she'd envisaged.

"What d'you think?" The subdued question burst out when she couldn't contain her anxiety a moment longer.

"Sophie, this is incredible. You must have spent days on this. And you're right about spending locally, too. I was planning to go with the people Arthur uses."

He turned the last page and looked up.

"I see they're all here, most of them asterisked."

"Then you don't mind my doing all this?"

"Mind! No way! I just wish I was as organised as you are. It's still over a year away, so I'm only now beginning to make concrete plans."

"That's all right then," Sophie heaved a sigh of relief. "I'm glad my work will be useful to you. We'll get as much done as possible while I'm here to help and I'll try to get back closer to the time to help then as well."

She unclipped a pile of handwritten pages joined concertina style and opened it out.

"I tried to work out which tasks can be carried out prior to the official start of the campaign and put them on a timeline. The rest of the dates will go on it when the Premier makes her announcement."

She pointed to the chart, Robert edging closer to read it over her shoulder, his arm along the top of the sofa behind her back. Sophie could feel the warmth of his body through her thin summer dress, and leaned into him to deepen the contact, her breath hitching in her throat and her pulse rate picking up.

When Robert suddenly straightened, putting space between them, she gritted her teeth, but let him go without protest, prosaically continuing to explain her chart.

"That red bar is the day the election date is announced and it all becomes official. Before then, you can be in unofficial electioneering mode, starting immediately with the rugby match this weekend." Sophie glanced up.

"Chat to as many people as you can, both local and visitors. Let them get to know you. They're all part of this electorate, aren't they? You can see I've made a list of upcoming events where you can meet and greet. You ought to write a few letters to the various editors on topical issues, too. Get your opinions on record."

"You're right, Soph. It's not too early to get a headstart. I'm glad you're here prodding me into action. Thank you. Will you let me make copies of these notes?"

"No need. This is your copy; I've got it all backed up on my laptop." She clipped the pages back into the folder and handed it to him. "Read through this lot, and tomorrow we'll put our heads together on what you ought to talk about on the weekend. We can have a test run down the pub on Friday night, if you don't have other plans."

I'm not really asking him on a date, she thought, but it would feel like one. And look like one, too. Which might give him a helpful nudge in the right direction.

"But... I..." Robert tried not to show how startled he was. It seemed he and Sophie had had vastly different ideas on the extent, and nature, of her promised help.

"I don't want to take up all your time, Sophie. That wouldn't be fair after all this work you've done for me."

"Rubbish! What really wouldn't be fair would be you kicking me off the campaign when I'm just getting my teeth into this electioneering gig. I intend to see you through to the end."

She turned in time to see him compose his face into a neutral mask, hiding what she was sure had been shock.

I was right, she thought. *He didn't take me seriously. Well, now he knows how very serious I am.*

"Remember? I told you I wanted to put this on my CV. Not much kudos in a job half done, is there?" While true, it wasn't anywhere near the whole truth, but his reactions warned her Robert wasn't ready to hear about her feelings for him. Feelings she wasn't yet one hundred percent sure of herself. She had detected definite signs of interest, despite the barriers he was erecting between them, and until she fully understood his reasons for holding himself aloof, she'd pretend to mere friendship.

"Anyway Rob, I'm tired. I've got a busy day tomorrow. I reckon it's time you pushed off. See you tomorrow night."

Sophie stood leaning against the doorjamb, watching Robert pick his way down the rutted lane in the dark, yawning behind her hand. No lie, she really was tired, but she felt satisfied she'd given that obstinate man something to think about besides his election campaign. She had impulsively kissed him goodnight as he left, letting him go almost immediately. It hadn't been her imagination that he'd returned her quick kiss.

I think I'll make a habit of kissing him, she thought, a cheeky grin up-turning her lips.

When he turned to wave on reaching the street, she waved back then switched off the outside light and locked up. After washing the coffee mugs, she paused to survey the kitchen, her hand on the light switch. Something was niggling at her memory. She'd been too excited to notice at the time, but something had upset Robert while she made the drinks earlier. Was it something she'd said, or…?

Her eye caught her mother's photo collection which he'd been studying. It was so much a part of the kitchen she rarely noticed it anymore, so she ran her eyes slowly over the rows. There. Another cheeky grin lit up her face. She hoped she was right. If he'd seen the picture of her and Gary and been jealous, then it meant he cared.

~~~~~

The next morning, Sophie bought a set of magnetic photo frames she'd seen in the shop and rearranged the fridge gallery, adding in several snaps of her own featuring her mother, and removing a couple of dated ones. Including the one of Gary, which was certainly outdated. She'd make a point of drawing Robert's attention to it when he arrived. Maybe a casual comment along the lines of 'D'you think Mum will mind me chucking out the old rubbish and rearranging her display?'

3

Robert gave the fridge gallery a quick glance when Sophie asked his opinion on what she had done, then looked again, more closely, when he didn't see the one photo he'd thought she would have made the focal point. It wasn't anywhere.

Because she included it among what she termed outdated rubbish, or because she put it somewhere more important? Private?

He was still mulling over the question in his mind when she tugged him down onto the sofa at her side to review yet another of her lists.

"Pay attention, Rob," Sophie commanded. "I've been talking to the customers today, finding out what issues the locals are up in arms about. I thought you could home in on them at the pub tomorrow night, and if they get people talking to you there, you could continue with them on Saturday at the rugby game."

Scanning the short list of topics Sophie handed him, Robert had to agree with her assessment of current issues, but his heart sank.

How he hated public speaking; in a casual, friendly arena almost as much as making a formal speech. Even his best friends got bored when he started talking. Hell, he even bored himself, and Sophie seemed to think this would be a regular part of his campaign. She was right of course, he thought glumly, but that didn't make it any more palatable.

"I don't know, Soph. Maybe all this talking isn't the best idea."

Sophie looked at him, wondering what his problem was. Politicians talked. It was part of the job. How did he imagine it could be avoided?

"It's just... You know. If I bore them to death, they're not going to vote for me when the time comes, are they?"

Taking in his obvious misery, Sophie recalled some of the snide comments she'd heard being bandied about behind his back. Suddenly she smiled, realising he'd misunderstood what she expected of him.

"Tell you what, Robert. We'll do a little role playing here. Pretend I'm Eddie Patterson. Talk to me about getting a Tidy Towns grant to build a bird hide down by the creek."

Robert sucked in a deep breath and started talking, only to be rudely interrupted a few moments later.

"No, no, no. Not you, Rob." Sophie grabbed his hands, pulling him to his feet. "She doesn't need *you* to tell her what's going on. Ask her what *she* thinks. What *she* wants. Your job is to get people talking, then listen. Try again."

It was as if the floodlights on the oval had been turned on in his brain.

Five minutes with Sophie and he knew where he'd been going wrong all these years. They practised a while longer, with Sophie being other people they were likely to meet, testing several other topics.

"By George, I think he's got it!"

Sophie punched the air, then flung her arms around him in a triumphant hug, spinning him round to sit beside her again on the sofa.

"Just remember, Rob. They talk; you listen. Slip in a question here and there to stir up the conversation. Show them what's important to them is important to you, too, and you won't go wrong."

She passed him the pen and notepad and leaned over his shoulder while this time he took notes as they talked enthusiastically. Robert was so buoyed up by the breakthrough he'd made with Sophie's help, he barely noticed how close she was until at last he threw down the pen and turned to face her; finding himself almost nose to nose with her.

Almost mouth to mouth.

For an interminable moment Robert was tempted to close the gap. His body let him know in no uncertain manner that was what *it* wanted. But this was his little Sophie, not some woman he might have a casual fling with. Carefully turning his eyes away, Robert took her gently by the shoulders and set her back on her end of the sofa.

For a moment Sophie had lost herself in the hazel depths of Robert's eyes. Her mind had gone blank, leaving her defenceless, yearning for him to close the gap.

Yearning to feel his lips on hers. When he set her aside, she almost whimpered, blinking rapidly to stem incipient tears.

Rising to his feet, Robert gathered up the notes they'd made, putting them into his briefcase, then picked up the coffee tray.

"C'mon Soph," he said when he judged himself capable of speaking nonchalantly. "I'll help you clear this lot up, then I'd better be going."

Obediently, Sophie followed him into the kitchen.

So close. She sighed.

He'd been so close to kissing her. She'd wanted that kiss so damn badly she could have screamed with frustration. A few minutes later she made very sure *she* claimed *a* kiss, if not *the* kiss, when she said goodnight.

"Sleep well, Rob. I'm really looking forward to seeing you in action tomorrow night."

Robert was too busy making his escape to notice the sly little smile twitching at Sophie's lips. She'd felt an unmistakable reaction just then, proving the man wasn't impervious to her, no matter how much he tried to pretend otherwise.

Which was just as well, as every time they were together, Sophie was more certain of her own deep emotional involvement. This time was nothing like her teen crush.

Ever the optimist, she was already planning her next romantic foray.

4

Sensing his nerves, Sophie clasped Robert's arm as they entered The Victoria Inn. Voices raised so conversations could be heard above the loud music blaring forth from the jukebox were an assault to their eardrums after the hushed quiet of the evening outside where the loudest noise was the mournful cry of a hunting mopoke or the occasional rumble of a vehicle crossing the bridge

They stood a moment getting their bearings.

"There."

Sophie nodded to the back corner where a group of people emerging from the dining room were pulling up chairs round a couple of tables hastily pushed together where it was a little quieter.

She tugged Robert along in her wake as she hurried over.

"Hello." She beamed her genuine pleasure at seeing them.

"D'you mind if we join you for a few minutes?"

Without waiting for a reply, Sophie claimed a chair beside Megan Armitage, pointing Robert to one across the table beside Alan Morgan.

"I'm so glad I caught you all tonight. Megan, I want to thank you for the lovely flowers you sent Mum. So many friends have called, all bearing flowers and pot-plants, so her room looks more like a florist's than a hospital."

Sophie chatted, answering questions about her mother's health, while noting out of the corner of her eye that Robert was laughing at something one of the men had said.

By the time the barmaid arrived to take orders, Sophie and Robert had been seamlessly incorporated into the group. When there was a lull in the conversation, Sophie gave Robert a miniscule nod, slanting her eyes towards Megan. Well coached, he picked up on her cue, leaning forward to be sure Megan heard his question.

"Megan, I wonder if you could explain something for me?"

"Happy to if I can, Bob."

"It's about this latest change in interest rates from the Reserve Bank. You're an accountant, so I thought you might be able to tell me how it's going to affect small businesses? Especially in country towns like The Crossing?"

Megan gave a concise, thoughtful answer to his question, then Geoff Tan complained about how the changes meant his bakery was being forced to put up prices. Alan backed him up, commenting on how Pete Hackett's bill for stock feed had gone up as well.

"So, is there anything we can do about it?"

Robert ventured another question, setting the conversation down another path. He listened, taking mental note of everyone's comments.

Then conversation became general once again when Elizabeth Tan asked if Megan's baby, Chloe, was teething yet.

Shortly after, Sophie jumped to her feet.

"There's Pam. Pam Lanner. We were best friends for years. Excuse me everyone, but I've got to go catch up with her. C'mon Rob."

With Sophie artlessly chatting up old friends, and Robert directing the conversation with a well-placed question or two, the two of them worked their way round the bar, garnering opinions on topics as diverse as coal seam gas exploration, to the market suitability of some of the new crops farmers were trialling.

In between conversational forays, Sophie hauled Robert onto the dance floor, ruthlessly ignoring his demurs, especially if a slow song was being played on the jukebox.

"This is so much fun, Rob, it's hard to remember we're working," she said, using the excuse of a crowded dance floor to snuggle a little closer in his arms. "I feel like Mata Hari, spying out important secrets."

"Umm. Mata Hari came to a bad end, didn't she? I wouldn't want that to happen to you, Soph."

Robert guiltily allowed himself to live in the moment, dancing cheek-to-cheek with his Sophie. It wouldn't last, but for a few minutes he could pretend. He was enjoying himself in the evening's mission, too.

Sophie's relaxed style of political meet and greet was surprisingly easy. Optimistically, he began to hope his long-held dream of a Parliamentary career might be achievable The music came to an end, replaced by something more upbeat. He reluctantly drew himself out of Sophie's arms. Looking around the room, he located another likely target.

Taking Sophie's hand, he led her over to the bar, claiming the last vacant stool for her. For the next few minutes, he stood comfortably behind her, chatting casually to Pete Hackett on one of their preselected topics. Drink finished, he leaned over Sophie's shoulder to put his empty glass on the bar.

"If you're ready, Soph, I think I've had enough. Joey's turned the volume up. Again. Let's get out of here before we go deaf."

"You're right. We've done what we came for and had a nice night out into the bargain."

Arms around each other, they walked along the street to Sophie's lane in a companionable silence, breathing in the scent of stocks and lavender growing in deep planters outside the shops. Sophie revelled in the rich feeling of happiness infusing her being. She rubbed her cheek against Robert's chest, inhaling the mingled scents of fabric softener, Imperial Leather soap and the dark, masculine essence exclusively Robert's own. Love bloomed in her heart as she thought how close she was to achieving her goal of sharing her life with this man. With Robert Whitman.

It wasn't far to her door. Not nearly far enough to satisfy Sophie's desire to walk on and on, arms holding each other close forever, but there wasn't much she could do about the geography.

If I'd been quicker, she thought, *I'd have suggested a walk down by the creek. With the moonlight glinting off the water, it could have been quite romantic. Another time,* she optimistically told herself. The night wasn't over yet.

Only it seemed it was.

While Sophie had been anticipating a pleasant hour or so snuggled up to Robert on her Mum's comfortable old sofa, reviewing the evening's successes, and more, if she had her way, he'd had other things on his mind.

Out of the pub, in the cool night air, Sophie had wrapped an arm around his waist, leaving him with no other option than to put his arm around her shoulders. It felt good, and that was the problem. It felt too good. How was he supposed to keep a respectable distance when she continually eroded his defences?

He didn't remember her being so…so tactile. As he recalled, little Sophie James had always been very shy with him. Now, it seemed, there wasn't a shy bone in her body.

How could a man be expected to keep his hands to himself with the woman who unfailingly inflamed his senses, forever touching him? Holding him, as she was right now? The delicate floral perfume she wore wreathed itself around his brain making it hard to concentrate.

From the beginning he'd had a bad feeling about letting Sophie help him. When he'd seen how productive her ideas were, he'd selfishly set his misgivings to one side. Now he realised he had to put their relationship back to the way it used to be before he crossed a line it was becoming harder and harder to discern.

"Home again. Let me get this door open, Rob, and I'll put the kettle on. I don't know why, but I always want a hot cuppa as soon as I get home."

Sophie, an inviting smile on her face, swung the door open, standing aside so Robert could follow her in.

"Er…No. I'm really not thirsty," he prevaricated, standing well back from the door. And that soft comfortable sofa of Dot's. He knew if he sat there beside Sophie tonight, he'd be lost.

"I need to get going, Soph. I want to jot down a few notes on tonight's discussions while they're still fresh in my mind."

"Good idea. I'll help."

"That's not necessary. You get a good night's sleep and I'll see you at the football tomorrow."

The smile disappeared from Sophie's face, leaving her staring at him as if she'd just been reprimanded. Robert hardened his heart and took another step back.

Towards safety.

What's wrong?

Sophie cast her mind back over the evening. Everything had been fine until they arrived on her doorstep. There was no reason she could come up with on the spur of the moment to explain what was going on, but it was clear Robert was dead set on making a speedy escape.

She'd thought he liked her. Maybe not to the same extent she liked… no, she'd be honest with herself, the way she loved him, but she'd been so sure he was leaning in that direction. She wanted to pound on his chest and shout at him.

She wanted to curl up in a ball and cry her eyes out. She needed time to sort out what she really, truly wanted from him. Needed from him.

Only it would never do to let him see how deeply he'd hurt her just now.

"Then I'll see you tomorrow," she agreed, through lips stiff with holding her emotions in check.

Maybe she'd been pushing too hard. Maybe she needed to back off and give him time and space to realise how important to his future wellbeing she was. Not for one minute would she give credence to the idea her feelings might not be reciprocated. Not when his responses to physical closeness between them told her otherwise.

"I'm visiting Mum after I close the shop tomorrow morning, so I'll probably be late." It was a spur of the moment sop to her pride, so she wouldn't look all clingy and needy.

"You go to the game as planned, and I'll catch you later on. Goodnight, Rob."

The alacrity with which Robert returned her farewell and hurried off without a backward glance, further lacerated her heart. By the time she'd locked the door, tears were flowing freely.

5

"What's the matter Darling?"

Dot studied her daughter's face, worry overlaying the lines pain had so recently etched into her gentle face. The girl had been a bit downcast during her afternoon visit, but she hadn't expected to see her again so soon. Especially on a Saturday night after the local rugby team had had a resounding victory. She should have been out celebrating with her friends instead of huddling by her mother's side trying to disguise her misery with a brave face.

"Oh Mum. It's nothing. You should be taking care of yourself, not worrying about me."

"If you don't tell me, I'll only worry all the more."

Sophie thought that quite likely. Her mother had always put her first, making all sorts of small sacrifices so she could have the opportunities Dot had never had. She probably would worry if she thought her child was in some sort of trouble. Besides, it had been at the back of her mind to confide in her mother when she impulsively decided to visit her for a second time that day.

"It's just... Mum, I'm just not sure what's best to do," she began, her hands clamped tightly together in her lap, eyes downcast. Then in a rush she spilled her heart out to her mother.

"It's Rob, you see. Robert Whitman. We've been spending a lot of time together this week while I've been helping him sort out his political campaign. I thought we'd gotten really close and I was so happy about it."

She risked a quick upward glance, reassured by her mother's encouraging smile.

"You know I've always had special feelings for him, don't you?"

Her mother nodded slowly.

"I know Darling. He's always had special feelings for you, too. In fact, there was a time during your teens when I feared for the two of you. He was too old for you, then. It might have really messed up your lives if he'd acted on what I could see he felt for you. I must admit, I was ever so relieved when he went back to university and you could go on being a care-free young schoolgirl."

Sophie nodded eagerly.

"Did you really think he felt like that about me?"

"Oh, there's no doubt about it at all. Hazel and I were both on tenterhooks for weeks. But Darling, it was several years ago. What's upsetting you now?"

"Well. I think... No, not think. I'm sure. Those special feelings have grown into love. On my side at least. I love the dumb idiot, Mum"

Dot's lips twitched, but she managed to keep a serious expression in place.

"All men have moments of dumb idiocy. What's Robert's excuse?"

Sophie jumped to her feet and began pacing in the narrow confines of the hospital room.

Dot's eyes glanced sideways towards her phone on the bedside table. Her fingers itched to snatch it up and call Rob's mother, Hazel. She was going to be verrry interested in this development, but Sophie hadn't got to the bottom of her story yet.

Seething with frustration, Sophie flung herself back down in her chair.

"Well," she said. "I was positive my feelings were reciprocated. Positive he just needed a bit of a nudge to wake up to the fact. So, I've been giving him lots of nudges, and everything was going really well. I thought. Now all of a sudden, he's backing off as if I've got some contagious disease or something. When I caught up with him at the football this afternoon, he deliberately evaded being alone with me. Just as he did last night. Mum, he treated me as if I were some importunate juvenile! How can I convince him I love him if he won't let me get close to him?"

"Hmmm."

Her daughter had never before come to her for advice on affairs of the heart. Dot wasn't sure what she should say, now she was confronted with this situation.

Unlike her friend Eddie Patterson, she firmly believed young people should be left to make their own decisions in matters of the heart.

"You know, Sophie," she cautiously ventured an answer. "Robert is a very reserved man. He takes his time over important decisions, and you've only been home for a week."

"You think I've been pushing too hard?"

"Maybe."

"I was afraid that might be the case, Mum. It's just... just so hard, knowing what I want and having to pussyfoot around because *he* isn't ready. It's not as if we're strangers or anything. We've known each other forever."

The disgruntled expression on her daughter's face almost made Dot laugh. Patience had never been one of her Sophie's virtues.

"Maybe that's part of the problem, Dear."

"Okay," Sophie muttered, her mind running hell-for-leather along this new track, trying to figure out her mother's meaning.

"I'll try not to rush him. Thanks Mum."

Sophie leaned forward and kissed her mother's cheek. For the remainder of her visit the interesting subject of Robert Whitman was shelved, their conversation turning to what they would do together when Dot was allowed home.

~~~~~

After church the next morning Sophie hung back, chatting to her own friends while patiently watching Robert out of the corner of her eye.

Her natural instinct had been to rush up to him and hang on his arm, tacitly claiming him as her man. That's what she would have done before Friday night. She wanted the whole world to see they belonged together, but his behaviour this weekend made her unnaturally diffident.

When, finally, she saw him signalling to his mother that he was ready to leave, she made her way across the churchyard, meeting up with them near the lychgate.

"Auntie Hazel. Rob."

She greeted her mother's best friend with her usual hug and kiss, blandly extending the same courtesy to Rob. She was careful not to go overboard, pretending she didn't notice his awkward blush, or the way he stepped aside as soon as she released him.

"Auntie Hazel," addressing his mother, Sophie turned her back on Robert as if he was of no account.

"I'm so glad I caught you before you got away this morning I just had to share my good news. Mum's making excellent progress. She thinks Doc Rogers will allow her home tomorrow."

"Wonderful, Sophie Dear. I'll pass it on to all her friends."

"I suppose that means you'll be off again any day now."

"Oh no, Rob." Sophie was pleased to detect a less than cheerful note in his voice. "Mum'll be too weak to cope on her own for ages yet. It's only because I'm here Doc's willing to let her home so soon. I'll still help you, whenever I've got time, but Mum comes first."

She directed a beaming smile Robert's way.

"I'll comb through the papers every day for new issues with local significance. Why not pop round after work one day to pick up my notes?"

Hazel silently absorbed every nuance of the interaction between her son and her best friend's daughter, amused at the girl's assumed nonchalance. Dot, who'd already brought her up-to speed on the latest development, would demand a full accounting next time they spoke.

She glanced to her side where another of her friends had paused, idly fussing over something in her handbag. She wasn't alone in paying careful attention to the young couple, Hazel realised.

"Hello Eddie. Reverend Charles gave a very interesting sermon this morning, didn't he?"

~~~~~

If she hadn't had the very real excuse of tending to her mother, Sophie didn't think she'd have been able to tolerate Robert's ominous silence.

By Wednesday morning she had formulated and discarded a dozen schemes designed to bring her to his notice in such a way he'd fall to his knees declaring undying love for her.

She sighed, remembering how Ben had raced to Geni's rescue when her life was in danger. Pity such dramatic events were unlikely to occur in her life. Not that she wished danger on either herself or Rob. Still...

Sophie gave herself a mental shake. She was far too pragmatic for silly daydreams. Or so she tried to convince herself.

Wednesday morning's newspaper provided her with an impeccable excuse to breach the invisible wall Robert had thrown up between them.

When Hazel Whitman arrived for a lengthy natter over the teacups with Dot, Sophie seized her chance. Tucking the paper under her arm, she stepped out briskly for Arthur Steedman's office.

If Robert wouldn't come to her, then she'd take matters into her own hands and beard him in his den.

She pushed open the door to the office, quickly taking in the three people with their heads together over a pile of papers scattered across one of the desks in the back of the room.

"Hello Mr Steedman; Betty; Rob. Am I intruding? I was hoping for a couple of minutes of Rob's time."

"Certainly you're not intruding." Betty Pascoe, another of Dot's close friends with her antenna finely tuned to romance, jumped in before either of the men could speak. "How's your Mum, Sophie?"

The social niceties out of the way, Sophie produced her newspaper, already folded to the correct page.

"You may have seen this already, Rob, but I brought it down in case you hadn't. One of your letters has been published."

All three crowded round her to read the letter to the editor she had circled in red.

"I like it Bob. A well-phrased, intelligent comment on that water rights issue we were discussing last week."

Arthur Steedman slapped Robert on the back.

"That's what I thought, too, Mr Steedman."

Sophie beamed, so pleased her opinion was being endorsed by a man whom she knew Robert respected.

"It ought to give the readers a good opinion of our Rob, don't you think? Being new on the political scene, he needs to raise his public profile well before the next election is announced, doesn't he?" Sophie rattled on artlessly, hoping Robert was taking due note of the respect Arthur was giving her ideas.

"When we discussed it last week, letters to the papers, like this one, was one of the ideas Rob suggested," she continued.

"Absolutely right, Sophie. Bob showed me the work you've been doing for him. You've got a good grasp on what's needed. He's a very lucky man to have a woman of your calibre behind him."

"This calls for a celebration," Betty announced, heading for the kitchen to put the kettle on. "You'll stay, won't you Sophie?"

"Actually Betty, I better be getting back. Rose is on her own in the shop, and if I'm away too long, Mum will be in helping her, and Doc says she's to rest. I just got excited when I saw Rob's letter and couldn't resist running over to show him."

"Thanks Soph. I'll see you out, then."

Robert's alacrity in getting rid of her brought out the worst in Sophie. She deliberately dawdled in the open doorway.

"Another thing, Rob." She turned to face him, hand on his arm, a bland smile hiding her annoyance. "I've finished the biography on you as I said I would. Can you pop round after work to proof-read it?" She glanced up at him from beneath her lashes before finishing up.

"Then I can send it in to the People and Events page. The editor thinks he can fit it in next week, but you have to approve it first."

"Oh. Well. I'm pretty busy," he began. When Sophie raised her brow, her expression turning slightly sceptical, he relented.

"Okay, Sophie. I guess I can spare five minutes. See you then."

He urged her forward, but before he could close the door behind her, she rose up on her tip-toes and kissed him. On the mouth, taking her time about it. In full view of Arthur Steedman and Betty Pascoe standing in the back of the office. And also in full view of Eddie Patterson and Carol Tan who happened to be passing by.

Sophie grinned to see him blush, but made a quick get-away before he rallied his defences.

"Bye Rob. See you tonight," she called over her shoulder as she hurried off.

She still wasn't sure what his problem with her was, but she was prepared to fight for her future happiness with whatever weapons came to hand.

Back at home, she looked in on her mother and Hazel telling them about her little expedition down the street. Not quite everything, but enough.

"Rob's coming round tonight to vet the bio I wrote on him. Probably straight after work."

Dot's phone rang just then, so Sophie went across to the shop to help Rose, leaving her mother and Hazel Whitman to finish their morning tea.

"Carol, how nice of you to ring."

Hazel could only hear Dot's end of the conversation with Carol, but it was enough to spark her interest.

"Really, Carol. Right out on the footpath, in front of you and Eddie? I bet she loved that. Wish I could have seen Rob's face, getting sprung by Eddie."

Dot laughed, listened again, then hung up.

"Guess what our kids have been up to Hazel?"

But Hazel didn't have to guess; Dot spilled the story with no urging at all.

"Do we dare play Cupid and help the kids out?" Hazel asked. "If we don't, Eddie will be cooking something up, and they're ours. Just once I'd like to get in first."

~~~~~

When Sophie came in to fix lunch for herself and her mother, she found Dot sitting in front of the TV, a guilty look on her face. Her immediate thought was that her mother had been overdoing things, but before she could open her mouth, Dot beat her to it.

"I hope you don't mind, Darling, but I've invited a dinner guest for tonight. I rang the butcher's and Bill sent some lovely lamb chops round. Rob likes his lamb, Hazel said."

"Rob... You've asked Rob to dinner?"

"That's right Dear. I hope it doesn't make too much work for you."

"He's coming then?"

"He demurred a bit, but Bill and Hazel are going away for a couple of days. He was going to get something from the takeaway, but I persuaded him to eat with us, since he has to look over your work anyway."

Sophie didn't know whether to thank her mother or scold her for interfering. She settled for an ambiguous kiss on the cheek.

"It's okay Mum. I'll make an apple pie for dessert."

But as for that man who could barely bring himself to give her five minutes, then about turned and willingly accepted her mother's dinner invitation ...

Well. She'd see about that! She'd like to shake him. Hard. Till his teeth rattled, Sophie thought. She was through waiting for him to realise he loved her and do something about it. The man needed shaking up and she was just the woman to do it.

~~~~~

"For you, Dot," Robert said, handing his hostess a bouquet of bright, sunny orange and gold calendulas. The flowers were accompanied by a kiss on the cheek.

"It's lovely to see you making such a speedy recovery."

Sophie, left to close the door behind him while he greeted her mother, had time to consider her response when presented with the second bouquet in Robert's arms; this one roses and gerberas in a soft, romantic pink. As the only other person present, they had to be for her.

It was the first gift of any kind he'd given her since he gave her a colouring book for her sixth birthday.

47

Even knowing he probably wouldn't have thought of bringing her flowers except that he had brought some for her mother as well, she couldn't help her militant attitude softening just a little.

He wasn't the enemy after all. He was the man she planned to spend her life with.

"These are an inadequate thank you for all your help, Sophie."

Robert handed the pink bouquet to her and stepped in close to buss her cheek as he had her mother's, but Sophie was having none of that.

At the last minute she turned her head so his lips landed fully upon hers and she used her free arm to pull him into a close embrace. His unmistakable response sent her pulse rate up a notch, and she smiled mistily at him when she stepped back, releasing him from her arms.

"Thank you. The flowers are lovely Rob, but helping you is a pleasure, not a chore."

Sophie noticed Robert looked even more embarrassed at being kissed in front of Dot than he had that morning in his office doorway. Taking pity on him, she turned to her mother giving him a moment to recover

"Mum, if you give me yours I'll pop all these flowers in a bucket of water till later when I have time to arrange them properly. Rob, before we eat, I want to show you the bio I mentioned this morning. It won't take long."

"No Dear," her mother surprised her with a surreptitious wink.

"I'll arrange the flowers while you and Robert talk business. If you'll just reach up and hand me the blue vase for mine and that crystal one for Sophie's, please Robert."

She opened her display cabinet and indicated the vases she wanted.

As promised, it only took a few minutes for Robert to review and approve the article she'd written. Not that he recalled a word of it five minutes later.

His mind was still in a whirl. He'd tried to do the gentlemanly thing and not take advantage of what he still thought was a mere crush, but Sophie ignored all his efforts. A selfish inner voice urged him to take what she was offering with all those kisses. He wanted her. Not just for the here and now. He wanted her for the long haul. He wanted her for his wife, no doubt about it, but still... The realisation staggered him, even though he'd had ample warning of the direction in which his feelings had been leading him.

All through the meal, he kept a weather-eye on Dot, wondering what she thought about a possible relationship between himself and her daughter, but it seemed she hadn't taken exception to what had transpired in front of her. If anything, she had been mildly encouraging.

Later, while Robert helped Sophie clear up after the meal, silence fell between them. A silence which grew uncomfortably long for Robert, driving him to fill it with words. He began by passing on to her Arthur Steedman's praise following her departure that morning.

Without thinking, he gave her the unexpurgated version. Verbatim.

"He was really taken with you, Soph. So much he even told me I'd be a fool not to marry you. He's been telling me for ages I need a wife..."

Sophie squealed, then flung herself upon him, wrapping her arms around his neck and kissing him more intimately than on his arrival. She was so engrossed she didn't hear the tinkle of breaking glass, but it was enough to bring Dot at the run, arriving in time to see her daughter lean back in Robert's arms. In time to hear her words following their kiss.

"Yes! Yes! Yes! Of course I'll marry you, Robert Darling. I've been in love with you for ages, hoping you loved me too."

"Oh dear. I'm sorry to come barging in." Dot went to leave, but Sophie let Robert go to grab her mother round the waist and dance her round in a circle.

"Rob asked me to marry him, Mum. Be happy for us."

In the background Robert made an inarticulate protest neither woman noticed.

"I am happy for you, Darlings, truly I am, but did you really need to break one of my favourite glasses?" She gestured to the broken glass on the floor beside the open dishwasher.

"Oops!" Sophie laughed, too happy to be distressed over a mere broken glass. "Sorry Mum. I was so excited I forgot it was in my hand."

Dot turned to Robert, backed up into the corner of her small kitchen.

"I couldn't be happier, Robert. I know you're the perfect husband for my girl." This time she was the one hugging and kissing him.

Stunned, Robert didn't utter a word. He didn't have to; between them, Sophie and her mother said everything that needed to be said, and more.

"It's hard to believe it was only this morning Your mother and I were saying what a lovely couple you two make."

Hard to believe indeed. Rob winced inwardly.

Dot phoned his mother with the news, claiming Hazel would want to know immediately, and after she'd had her say and pushed the phone into his hand, his parent's congratulations rang loudly in his ears.

It was too late to explain he hadn't meant his words as a proposal.

Robert thought he heard derisive laughter from his inner man.

He was an engaged man. Without having done or said a thing. He wasn't sure whether he felt like laughing or crying.

6

"What's the matter, Bobby?"

Tony Whitman leaned against the veranda rail, his attention centred fully on his younger brother. Music and the muted sound of numerous voices wafted from the main part of the house, but it was quiet in this corner where he'd led Bobby for a private chat.

In the midst of the family celebration of Bob's engagement to Sophie James, it struck him his brother stood out as being less enthusiastic than one would expect in a man who'd just attained his heart's desire.

And, Tony knew, Sophie really was the subject of Bob's desire. She always had been. It had caused him severe misgivings when, some years earlier the brother he was so proud of came to him confessing to being in love with the twelve-year-old child Sophie had been then. Time had eventually erased that impediment, though, without altering his brother's attachment to the girl by one iota. By rights, Bob ought to be over the moon.

"Nothing." Robert responded instantly with a prickly denial. "Why would you think anything's wrong, Tony?"

"C'mon Bro. This is me you're talking to. I know you as well as I know myself. Share the load."

Robert huffed and maintained his denial of trouble, but not for long. His big brother had always been his go-to man when he needed advice.

"It's just... I don't know Tony. Everything happened so fast. One minute I was helping Sophie clear up after dinner, telling her how Arthur reckoned all good politicians need a wife, and next thing she's saying she accepts my proposal. Then Dot was in one the act, and the parents. Before I knew it, Mum's throwing this engagement party for us."

Tony nodded at him to continue. Robert lowered his eyes.

"It was all a big mistake, Tony." Almost under his breath he finished his explanation. "I never asked her to marry me at all. She jumped in before I finished speaking, and the next minute we're engaged."

"O-kay. I get what happened. Do you want to call it off? Because I'm telling you Bro, the longer you leave it the worse it'll be."

Only my brother could make a monumental stuff-up like this! Tony had to work at not laughing out loud.

"No." Robert visibly shuddered. "I'd be better off dead than pulling a stunt like that."

"Maybe. But you know, Bobby, the rest of your life's a long time to live with a mistake."

"It's not really a mistake. Exactly. It's just… I'm too old for a kid Sophie's age. I'd decided to get out of her way and let her find someone more appropriate, but now she's stuck with me. What if she comes to regret jumping into marriage so impulsively? D'you think I ought to tell her?"

"Hmm. Once your age difference was a huge problem, but it's sought of evened out by now, don't you think? If that's all that's bothering you, I'd say keep the mistake under your hat and take the gift the gods have granted you. If you do want to marry her, that is."

He slapped his brother on the back and headed round the veranda to the door, hoping his quixotic little brother wouldn't do anything completely idiotic.

~~~~~

Hearing footsteps approaching, Sophie turned tail and scurried inside a split second before Tony rounded the corner. Ducking into a darkened bedroom to avoid detection, she sank into a huddle on the floor, her hands over her face. Tears seeped from her eyes, and she struggled to hold in her sobs.

It wasn't true, what she'd overheard when she went looking for Robert. It couldn't be, except it must be. She'd heard Robert say it himself. He hadn't meant his words as the lead-up to a proposal. He didn't want to marry her, but he'd been trapped, and was too kind to say otherwise.

This wasn't the way she wanted to get married. If Robert didn't love her, didn't want to marry her, then she'd put her own feelings aside and call it off. Now. Tonight. It would be the shortest engagement in Oxley Crossing's history, but she'd do what was right and count the cost later.

There was no time like the present, so she wiped her eyes on a corner of her skirt and resolutely pushed herself to her feet. Once more she went outside in search of her fiancé.

~~~~~

"Rob. We need to talk."

Mindful of how she herself had overheard a private conversation, Sophie tugged impatiently on his arm, leading him to a seat under the gumtree at the bottom of the yard. A seat with a clear view of anyone approaching them.

"Sophie! What do you mean? We're always talking, aren't we? What's so urgent we need to discuss it in the middle of our party?" Although something about her solemn demeanour and abrupt demand they talk was giving him the cold shudders. Sophie had sounded unnaturally grim just now. Surely Tony wouldn't have said anything to her?

Sophie hesitated, unsure of how to begin, then threw caution to the winds and dived right in.

"I heard you talking to Tony just now. Did you really not intend to ask me to marry you?"

"Well... Maybe not right then, but..."

"So it's true."

"Only partly. I would have got round to asking you sooner or later."

"Would you?"

Robert broke into a cold sweat. Cynicism, directed towards himself, was so uncharacteristic of the Sophie he was used to, he was left floundering.

"I inadvertently trapped you into this engagement, didn't I?" She didn't wait for an answer to what was a purely rhetorical question.

"I'm sorry Rob. It'll cause a bit of a stink, but I'll put things right. I don't think I'll be able to help you any more with preparing for the election, and I'm sorry for that, too. As soon as Mum's back at work, I'll be off. You won't have to put up with bumping into me everywhere you go."

She sprang to her feet, blinking hard to stem incipient tears, and grabbed his hand.

"C'mon. Let's get this over with. Just follow my lead, Rob. I'll take all the blame since I caused the problem in the first place. There'll be an outcry, but in the end, it'll be no more than a nine days wonder. Silly Sophie James who doesn't know her own mind."

At a near run, she set off for the veranda dragging Robert along in her wake.

Until he literally dug in his heels, hauling her up in front of him, both hands securing her so she couldn't escape.

"Just hang on a moment, Soph. You're going off half-cocked with the wrong end of the stick." He knew he was mixing his metaphors but getting his point across was more important than good English.

"I haven't had my say, so get back on that seat and listen to me." He dragged her back to the garden bench, and frantically tried to get his thoughts in order.

Mutinous, but not in the least cowed, Sophie clamped her lips together and stared him down.

"Let's back up a bit, Sophie. Yes, it's true I didn't actually propose the other night, but that doesn't mean I didn't intend to. I did. I love you Sophie. I have for years, ever since you were a kid. Only you really were too young then. Being in love with you made me feel I was some kind of pervert, so I blocked you off in my mind as forbidden territory, then we didn't see each other for a long time. I didn't realise you'd grown up, and I suppose it's taken me a while to break through that barrier."

He rubbed his hands over his face, looking through his fingers to see her response. *Not good,* he thought. She sat on the bench, impassive as an Easter Island statue.

"I don't move at the speed of light the way you do, Soph. I wasn't ready on Wednesday night, but I was getting there. If you hadn't been so impatient, you'd have got your proposal. As romantic a one as I could manage. I want to marry you, Sophie James, and I really, really don't want to call our engagement off. I really don't."

He sat down beside her and took her hands into his, willing her agreement.

"You're not just saying all that in some misguided act of chivalry, are you?"

It was almost a relief to hear the tremor in her voice. It meant he was getting through to her. He hoped. The tight knot in Robert's chest, eased slightly.

"I'm really not, Sophie. Please say you'll stay engaged to me," he begged.

Sophie thought over all he'd said. A lot of it had hurt, but some had been surprisingly sweet.

She'd thought herself too pragmatic to need pretty words, but maybe she'd been wrong. Also, there'd been a ring of truth in his words. Some of them, at least.

Decision made, she looked up, meeting him eye-to-eye.

"Apart from saying you love me, I think one of the most important things you just said was that you're not really ready to marry me yet. You sounded as if you still have issues from when I was just a kid. That must have been awfully hard for a young man to cope with, Rob. Therefore, I'll agree to a compromise. I'll take the whole matter of our engagement under advisement and stay engaged to you, going on as normal, except there'll be no talk of marriage till you convince me you're over all your hang-ups. We won't set a date. Won't make any plans at all. If, in the meantime, you decide you want out, say so. Otherwise I'll wait till I'm sure you're ready."

It wasn't precisely what he wanted, but it gave him a breathing space to correct his mistakes. The air whooshed silently from his lungs as he finally relaxed.

As to Sophie's compromise offer, Robert's reply was to take her in his arms and seal his reprieve with a kiss that felt like a solemn vow. He felt her resistance weaken, her lips losing their rigidity under the gentle persuasion of his. He stroked his tongue softly over them, feeling them part to admit him to the sweetness of her mouth.

"Hey you two lovebirds, Aunt Hazel wants you inside to cut the cake," yelled Robert's young cousin, Johnny.

They drew apart with a breathless laugh.

"Okay, Soph?"

"Okay Rob. Let's go slay the cake."

"Just as long as it's not my heart you're slaying," Robert whispered.

7

It was barely a week after the engagement party when Doc Rogers gave Dot the all-clear, permitting her to return to work. Sophie rejoiced for her mother, of course, only it left herself with way too much time on her hands. And time on her hands was the worst situation possible for a chronic workaholic. It gave her time to doubt herself; to question every decision she'd made over the past month or two. It sapped at her confidence.

She had loved spending time with her mother, but now she itched to get back to some real work, except to do so would mean leaving The Crossing again; something she wasn't willing to do with the uncertain state of her engagement to Robert.

Lately he'd been all she could wish for in a suitor. Now, it was Robert who pulled *her* into his arms for kisses when they met or parted. Robert who instigated love-making when they were alone, even when it interfered with the work she was doing for him.

He brought her flowers and chocolates. and took her on dates. Real dates, not meet and greet sessions to further his ambitions, although there were some of those, too.

In a truly romantically staged moment one evening he slipped a ring of his own choosing on her engagement finger, overruling her token protest. Token, because the ring was so perfect. A unique twin hearts setting of two rare pink diamonds from Australia's Argyle mines. If the engagement eventually came to nothing, she'd have trouble returning it.

"Oh, Rob," she'd whispered, melting into his arms. "It's absolutely perfect. I love it."

"Enough to make our engagement real and set a date?"

Sophie had frozen, her tender mood shattered.

"I hadn't pegged you as the manipulative type, Robert Whitman."

She tugged at the ring which had been on her finger for so short a time. He ought to know she couldn't be bought.

"No! No Sophie." Robert reached to stay her impulsive action. "Don't take it off. I didn't mean it the way you're thinking."

The beautiful ring stayed on Sophie's finger, but their date came to a premature end, Robert in a huffy temper which in a less equable man might have erupted into outright anger. Guilty but adamant, Sophie shed angry tears when she finally reached the sanctuary of her bedroom.

The weeks since her engagement party had seen Sophie's world first rocked on its axis, then sliding rapidly downhill. She prided herself on being decisive; on knowing her own mind, and here she was dithering over the simplest of choices; like what to bake for morning tea. The current unsatisfactory situation was killing her.

When something was right, the different pieces usually clicked into place with the ease of fitting a jig-saw together. In loving Rob, most of the pieces fitted perfectly. It was only when she tried to add marriage to the board she ran into trouble. It looked like the right piece, but it just wouldn't sit right. Her mind worried at the problem, round and round, achieving nothing.

"Damn it all," she cursed under her breath, impatient with the unaccustomed introspection.

Impulsively she threw down the duster she'd been wielding on the already pristine surfaces in her mother's lounge room and set off to see if Robert was free for lunch. At the last minute, she rushed back to the kitchen and filled a plate with chocolate brownies she'd baked that morning, hoping the peace offering would help smooth things over between them. Chocolate worked for her; she crossed her fingers hoping it would have a similar effect on her fiancé.

~~~~~

"Hello." Sophie breezed into the office. Robert was on the phone, so she dropped a kiss on his forehead, deposited the brownies on his desk, and went across to the work bench where Betty was stuffing envelopes, automatically reaching out to help with the mundane task.

"Got a moment Sophie?" Betty smiled her thanks, continuing, "I was going to call you when I finished this. Now you've saved me the trouble. Put the kettle on, will you? We'll have a cuppa out the back and talk. Bob's likely to be a while yet."

Thinking nothing of Betty's request, Sophie did as asked. It came as a surprise to discover there was a purpose behind it.

"You're at a loose end, aren't you Sophie? Would you be interested in a well-paid online job, working from home?"

"I'm unemployed. I'll consider any reasonable offer, Betty."

"That's what I hoped. This job has the added advantage of being portable. After you and Bob are married, you'll be able to pick up and go with him without it interfering with your work."

"Sounds good. Tell me what's involved."

"My niece gave up her executive position with one of the big advertising firms when she married a farmer. She did a few little jobs for friends of his, then realised country businesses had a genuine need for someone with her tech skills, but there wasn't enough local work to warrant opening an office." Betty slowed for a breath, then carried on.

"She came up with the idea of an on-line office catering to people all over the country. It's taken off like a rocket. Now she's recruiting extra staff; independent, capable women like herself, to expand the business. When I told her about you, she begged me to give you her address and ask you to email if you're interested."

"I am interested. If this pans out, it'll be just what I need, now and in the future. Thanks Betty."

During the several exchanges following this discussion, Betty's niece, Amanda Pierce, and Sophie agreed on a face-to-face meeting in Nyngan, the nearest town to where Amanda lived.

With butterflies in her stomach, Sophie set off early in the morning three days later. Not that she need have worried.

She took an instant liking to Amanda, although she couldn't recall a more rigorous interview. However, it proved worth it.

She left Nyngan with a generous contract and enough client accounts to keep her busy, with the assurance there'd be as many more to come as she could handle when these were fulfilled. It was an entirely new career direction, but one she rather thought she would enjoy more than a conventional nine-to-five office job. She'd be setting her own hours, and the work promised to be both varied and interesting.

Suddenly those jig-saw pieces comprising her life were once again falling into place, one after the other in rapid succession. She found herself eagerly compiling new lists, planning for the future on the drive home.

~~~~~

"Mum. Rob." Sophie looked from one to the other that evening as she caught them up on the outcome of her trip to Nyngan.

"I'm so excited I can hardly wait to set up my computer and get started. I was beginning to worry over finding something suitable, then this just fell into my lap."

"That's wonderful Dear. I'll move my stuff out of the den and you can use it till you and Rob set up a home of your own."

Which reminds me... thought Robert. In all the drama over their engagement, neither he nor Sophie had given a thought to where they would live if... *When,* he amended, when they eventually married.

Shortly after, he brought the subject up again while sharing a celebratory drink with Sophie at the pub.

"I know you said you're not ready to make wedding plans, Soph, but several years ago I bought a building block across the creek when the Murchison property was broken up. What do you say to helping me build a house on it? It's high time I got a place of my own. I'm fed up with living in a pokey little flat at the back of my parents' house," he added, forestalling any protest she might make.

"If we make a start on it now, it will save time later," he urged, fingers crossed she wouldn't take exception to his tacit assumption. Just lately he'd found himself walking on eggshells around this woman he loved. He wondered if maybe he ought to take a stand, only a little voice in the back of his mind continued to sound a warning. Sophie could be led, he'd discovered, but any attempt to drive her had her digging her heels in.

Running her finger slowly round the rim of her glass, Sophie considered the merits of his suggestion. Truthfully, she'd been tempted more than once to put an end to her embargo on the wedding and take a chance they'd be happy together. Especially since Robert had been working so assiduously to convince her of his commitment. She didn't know why she'd dithered for so long. Collaborating in building a house, they'd be building for a shared future. The future she longed for.

"Okay, Rob," she agreed. "That sounds like fun. Do you have any ideas on what you want?"

The remainder of the evening they spent drawing plans on the back of coasters, arguing over the number of bedrooms and bathrooms the house ought to have, and whether it should be one or two stories, how ecologically sustainable it should be, and other, equally important, issues.

That evening Sophie returned Robert's goodnight kisses with passionate abandon. Hearing Dot's cuckoo clock call the hour, Robert reluctantly drew back, preparing to leave. Dot's porch swing lacked both the comfort and privacy for where they were headed if he didn't call a halt, he thought. If Sophie had been living on her own, he would have asked to stay. He didn't think he was being too conceited in believing that tonight she would have agreed. His heart lifted, sensing she was close to granting him all he wanted.

Closer than he realised.

"Rob…" Sophie snuggled up to him, her arms wrapped around him, holding him in place. She felt the rapid thud of his heart beating in unison with her own. Looking up, she fastened her eyes on his.

"You've been very attentive since the party. Are you really as happy about getting married as you seem to be?"

"I am, Soph. I've tried everything I know to convince you. I don't know what else I…"

Sophie placed her fingers across his lips to silence his protest.

"Darling, you have convinced me," she murmured. Removing her fingers from his lips, she replaced them with her lips.

Later, much later, when they came up for air, Robert whispered, "How soon, Sophie Darling? I don't want to wait forever. Do you think you could make it soon?"

Struggling into an upright position, Sophie reached for her bag and retrieved her phone, taking his request literally.

"Let's see. If we get a marriage licence soon as, then one month's notice… Here we are." She scrolled through her calendar, checking her Saturdays. "This is the earliest free Saturday, Rob. Eight weeks from this weekend. Any sooner we'll have to book a week day which will be horribly inconvenient for most of our guests."

Robert had also been scrolling through his appointments. He compared calendars and agreed the date, his mind in a whirl as always seemed to be the case when his Sophie made decisions in her inimitable style.

"Now we hope Reverend Charles can fit us in. I'll try the Bowling Club for the reception. It'll be tight, Rob, but doable. Oh, Rob. I'm so excited. Eight weeks and four days till we're married!"

~~~~~

By Friday night, after speaking to Reverend Charles on Thursday morning, the church was booked, and, Sophie reported, the Club auditorium was also. Dot had ordered in a special shipment of the invitations they had chosen from her catalogue. It had been delivered just before closing time and Sophie had already made serious headway on filling them in.

Pam Lanner, consulted via Skype, had been thrilled to be asked to be bridesmaid, and she and Sophie had agreed on colours and styles for their dresses. A shopping day, with Dot and Hazel included, was planned for the following week.

"So, flowers, menus and music to go and we'll be home and hosed with weeks to spare. Mum and I hope to get the invitations in the mail on Monday. How about you, Rob?"

"On target. Tony will be my best man. Suits are in the pipeline. Photographer's booked. I'm looking into honeymoon locations, and Darling, an extra bit of good news. Mum and Dad booked themselves onto a round the world cruise to celebrate their retirement. They'll be leaving a month after the wedding and want us to house-sit for them, so we won't have to cram into my tiny flat for long at all. By the time they get home, our house will be almost finished."

"Wonderful! Who said a wedding takes months and months to organise?"

"What did you decide about the house you're building for yourselves?" Dot asked. "Will you be putting it on hold till after the wedding?"

Robert chuckled, while Sophie laughed outright. A laugh brimful of joy and confidence.

"No way, Dot. Don't you know your own daughter by now? She's never happier than when faced with an impossible schedule. Right now, she must be in seventh heaven with her new job and our wedding. Organising builders is the cherry on top. She's not even letting me slack off on my informal political meetings."

"Certainly not!" A pensive expression flitted across Sophie's face. "Rob, am I being too pushy? I really don't mind what career you choose, you know. I just want to help you succeed in whatever makes you happy."

"Which is exactly what you are doing, Darling. Your enthusiastic support is *my* cherry on the top." He leaned over to kiss her lightly, then straightened to address Dot who was sitting on the other side of the kitchen table.

"You asked about the house, Dot. We've decided on doing it the easy way, since on-site builders have to be imported and their accommodation for months on end added to the overall costs. On Monday we've got an appointment with a Tamworth company building those relocatable homes like the one George Anderson built for his son when he got married a couple of years ago. They build it on their lot, then truck it in sections to be assembled on our land when it's done. Less than a week on site here, and all we need to find is a plumber and electrician to connect us to the mains. They have some great floor plans and it means we'll have our own brand-new home before Christmas. A huge bonus is, Mum and Dad offered us the same low-interest loan they gave Tony, so we won't be at the mercy of the banks for years to come."

"Well, my dears, if it's true the Devil finds work for idle hands, you two are definitely in the hands of the angels." Dot smiled mistily, so happy her hopes for her daughter were being realised.

If only... she thought wistfully, as she had many times over the years.

~~~~~

The very next day, Sophie's carefully constructed plans came under attack from an unexpected source.

The phone rang, and she answered, her mind more than half absorbed with setting up a website for a small, family-owned company selling farm machinery out the back of Bourke.

"Sophie, we need you to talk some sense into Bob." Sophie recognised Betty, who was thoroughly exasperated by the sound of it.

Quickly saving her work, she gave the call her full attention. Betty wouldn't be calling her for help over anything trivial.

"What about, Betty?"

"Parliament's sitting, as you know, and Arthur just rang from Canberra. June, his wife, has been diagnosed with early-onset Alzheimer's. He's decided to pull the plug. Immediately. He says she's supported him for years; now it's his turn to be there for her. He's offering to support Bob's candidacy if he decides to run in the Federal by-election his resignation will cause. He says the only reason he encouraged Bob to run for the State was so they wouldn't be up against each other. Now that won't apply any longer, he reckons Bob ought to set his sights on Canberra. The idiot's having trouble switching his ideas from running for State next year to the Feds immediately. Here, Soph, I'll hand you over to Bob."

Sophie heard a short, muttered conversation then Robert's voice sounded in her ear.

"I'm sorry, Sophie. Betty had no right interrupting your work…" Sophie cut in, not waiting for him to finish.

"She says you're undecided about whether or not to stand. It sounds like a wonderful opportunity to me, one that's not likely to come along again any time soon. You've got a head start already in what will be a very short campaign, judging by other by-elections. That's got to be to your advantage, Rob. If you wait for a general election, the big Parties will have time for saturation advertising you can't hope to match. Do you want to be in Parliament or not?"

"Yes! Yes, I do. It's just… Do you think I'm ready for this, Soph?"

"The question is, Robert Whitman; do *you* think you're ready? You won't be on your own, you know. Betty said Arthur's offering his support, and that will count for a lot. I'm behind you, too, and your family."

There was a long pause, then Sophie heard him release a pent-up breath.

"You're right, Soph. I'll do it."

"Good. Then get back to Arthur. I'll see you at lunchtime. Bye Darling."

By the time Arthur Steedman's resignation was made public early the following week, Robert, backed by Arthur and his support team, had his official campaign ready to be rolled out the instant the Speaker issued the writ for a by-election.

~~~~~

"Saturday the ninth!" Betty, monitoring the parliamentary broadcast, reported. "Nominations close Friday next week, then we go to the polls on the ninth. They're not wasting any time, are they?"

"The ninth! Betty, we can't do it. The wedding is on the ninth." Robert clutched his hair and paced a rapid circuit of the room.

"Bloody Hell, Betty! Sophie will have my head on a platter if we have to cancel."

"Oh Lord, you're right. Ring her. Now."

His heart in his mouth, Robert picked up his phone, then put it down again. He needed face-to-face for something this important.

"Hold the fort, Betty. I'll be back soon."

~~~~~

"The ninth! What'll we do Rob?" Sophie paled as her wedding plans threatened to come crashing down around her.

"As far as I can see, we'll either have to give up on the election, or postpone the wedding. Soph, I'm sorry. This is all my fault. I should have considered the possibility of the dates clashing."

Sophie stared at him, aghast. Everything was booked, deposits paid, and acceptances already coming in.

If she cancelled, and Rob got in as he had an excellent chance of doing, he'd be off to Canberra immediately. It could be months till he was free to reschedule the wedding. And scuttling his campaign was out of the question.

She paced restlessly round the kitchen, her mind racing. Swinging round to face Robert, she gulped in a deep breath, straightening her spine, determined not to falter.

"We'll do both, Darling. I'm not sure how yet, but I'll find a way. Let's both go back to work for now. I'll call a family meeting tonight and see if we can work out how it can be done."

Ten minutes later he was reporting back to Betty.

"We can lodge my nomination. Sophie reckons we can manage both and I'll hold her to it."

~~~~~

It was Marcia, Robert's sister-in-law, who tabled the most workable suggestion.

"The scheduling on the day will be awkward," she uttered pensively, "but I think if you move the time of the ceremony back as late in the afternoon as possible, and time the reception to begin after the polls close, Bob can still spend the day touring the polling stations to thank his supporters handing out how-to-vote materials, and still get home in time to front up at the church. What d'you reckon, Soph?"

"We'll do it. You're a genius Marcia." Sophie rounded the table to fling her arms around her future sister-in-law.

It wasn't the end of the discussion by any means, but Sophie tuned out most of the back and forth arguing, already making a new to-do list to work the change of time. On Monday she sent out a notice to their invited guests, cheekily adding an attachment telling them to

VOTE 1 – Robert WHITMAN (Independent).

After that, it was back to fitting frenetic wedding preparations into Robert's gruelling, fast-paced campaign.

8

While struggling a little with making speeches, Robert had felt he'd handled the question periods quite well. It was best when Sophie was beside him on the platform, silently encouraging him, but even when she couldn't be with him he felt confident after the first few times. He'd even stoically withstood the expected heckling from his opponents, foremost among whom was Paul Breen who sneeringly referred to Robert as 'Bob, the butcher's boy', but with nothing else worthy of the effort required, there was very little mud-slinging in the weeks leading up to the by-election.

Not until the Monday morning three weeks prior to Saturday the ninth.

A screaming headline caught her eye as Sophie helped her mother set out the daily papers early in the morning before Rose arrived for work.

CANDIDATE'S ABANDONED LOVE-CHILD

Beneath the attention-grabbing headline was a photo of a delightful, curly-haired toddler in a playground.

Wanting to finish up and head inside to make a start on her own work, Sophie almost ignored it. Recently it seemed every time she turned around there was some new scandal in Canberra, most of them hyped up to fever-pitch by the media then petering out after a week or two. Only this time it was the Tamworth paper read by most people in the region, not one of the national dailies. Besides, it read 'candidate'. Curious, she picked up the top copy to see who'd been caught out.

As she read, her knees buckled, and she found herself sitting in a trembling heap on top of the pile of newspapers, her stomach threatening to part company with her breakfast.

"Mum!"

Dot came running on hearing her daughter's strangled cry. Ashen-faced, Sophie mutely held out the newspaper. Dot quickly scanned the inflammatory front-page article which claimed that struggling single mum, Charlene Larsen, had named Robert Whitman as the father of her child.

"Oh dear," she exclaimed weakly. "I wonder if Rob knows about this?"

"Well, if it's true, I should think he most certainly does!"

Despite the nausea churning in her stomach, Sophie was beginning to rally, temper bringing the colour back to her cheeks.

"But if you mean, does he know it's front-page news, probably not."

"I don't believe a word of it." Dot had been carefully rereading the article, and now came down staunchly in favour of her future son-in-law.

"I bet it's a beat-up from that Breen fellow who's been sending hecklers to all Rob's public meetings. He had a bad case of sour grapes when Rob won their debate last week."

"I'm sure you're right, Mum, but there must be something to it, or they wouldn't have printed it."

"You shouldn't let it upset you Darling." Dot, helping her daughter to her feet, gave her a warm hug. Seeing she had failed to banish the wan, pinched look from Sophie's face, she tried again to offer consolation.

"He was a single man then, and it's all long over. Besides, Darling, who cares if this woman was once his girlfriend."

"That's not the point, Mum." Sophie, wiping her hands over her face, dismayed to find her cheeks damp, began to pace back and forth in front of the paper stand.

"It's the child, don't you see? Old girlfriends are to be expected, but a child is something else." She turned a pleading face towards her mother, throwing her hands out in a questioning gesture.

"What kind of man abandons his own child? I would never have credited Robert Whitman with such callous disregard for his responsibilities. If it's true, he's not the man I thought him to be. Have I made a dreadful mistake, Mum?"

"Sophie! Sophie, my dear. Don't go making important decisions in the heat of the moment. Who's to say the paper got it right? You know how some journalists make a dreadful mish-mash of the facts." Now it was Dot pleading with her daughter. Her mind struggled to cope with the probable outcome if Sophie acted precipitously.

Arrested by Dot's argument, Sophie came to an abrupt halt, staring into nothingness while turning the story over in her mind.

"Absolutely right, Mum. There's only two people who know the truth, and one's just down the street. I'm going to see Rob, and he'd better have a good explanation, or else…"

"Sophie! Sophie, come back."

Sophie slowed in the doorway, looking back at her mother.

"What?"

"Please, Darling. Don't go steaming in all fired up for a fight. Show him the paper, listen to what he says, and don't make any decisions in a hurry. Promise me, Sophie." Dot had rushed over to take her by the hand while making her plea.

Sophie considered for a moment, then nodded curtly.

"Okay, Mum. I'll listen, but it had better be good."

Knowing that was the best she could hope for at this point, Dot gazed agonisingly after her daughter as Sophie dashed off, rolled newspaper brandished at an aggressive angle. If there had been someone else to mind the shop, she'd have followed.

A few minutes later, Sophie was knocking on Hazel Whitman's kitchen door, having failed to run her quarry to ground in his own quarters.

"Good morning, Hazel. Is Rob here?" Her temper was still running high, but she reined herself in to greet her future mother-in-law pleasantly, if a trifle more abruptly than usual.

"Come on in, Sophie. Bob's just having breakfast with his father. Pull up a chair and I'll pour you a coffee."

"Thanks," Sophie muttered through horribly stiff lips. She stepped past Hazel into the breakfast nook. With no more than a curt nod to Bill, she fixed her eyes on Robert's face, striding into the room to take up a rather belligerent stance at his side.

When Robert made to rise, she put her hand on his shoulder, holding him firmly on his chair, too impatient for social niceties.

She also dodged his attempt to draw her down for a kiss, instead, slapping the folded newspaper onto the empty plate in front of him.

"You might want to take a look at this."

Alarmed, Robert stared at his normally affectionate fiancée. He could almost swear she'd ground her teeth when she spoke.

"What is it Darling?"

"Read it."

Clipped voice, tightly clamped lips and her stand-offish posture combined to warn Robert his love was in a raging temper, under very tight rein. He studied her warily, then slowly began unrolling the paper.

His mother, alerted by Sophie's unusual manner, leaned forward to read over his shoulder.

"No!" she gasped, hand to her heart. "Son, tell me it's not true!"

Bill Whitman, hastily swallowing his last mouthful of toast, heaved himself out of his chair and rushed to her side, reading the article over Robert's other shoulder.

"It better not be true!" he thundered. "I'll not stand for a son of mine treating any woman like this!"

79

Paradoxically, Bill's rage calmed Sophie. She quietly pulled out a chair and sat beside her fiancé, reaching for his hand.

"Bill. Hazel. Why don't we all sit down and let Robert tell us what it's all about? I'm sure there's a rational explanation," she said, offering a voice of reason in the face of the excess of emotion turning the breakfast table into a melodramatic stage.

And if there isn't, Sophie thought, *I'll be having my say in private, not in front of his parents over the remains of their breakfast.*

Half an hour later, Robert's convoluted explanations having run their course, Sophie recapped the story, omitting the numerous animadversions which had interrupted the initial telling.

"So, what you're saying, Rob, is that when you worked in Tamworth, this girl, Charlene Larsen, lived in the same block of flats?"

Robert nodded mutely, and Sophie continued.

"You knew each other, but you claim she wasn't ever your girlfriend, and there's no way her child could possibly be yours. Have I got that right?"

"Yes. I've told you the absolute truth, Sophie. We never so much as had coffee together, let alone go on a date. She's lying, Sophie. I don't know why, but I swear she is."

Anxiously, he waited for her reply, breaking out in a cold sweat when instant reassurance was not forthcoming.

After re-reading the offensive article, Sophie had yet another question.

"It says here, when she told you she was pregnant, you threw a teddy bear in her lap, 'for the baby' the reporter says, and hightailed it out of Tamworth so fast you couldn't be seen for dust. Did you give her a teddy bear? Then leave town?"

"Yes, but…"

He looked round the table, daunted by the sorrowful accusation on the faces of both his parents. Sophie's deadpan expression felt even worse. It sickened him to realise even so simple a gesture as a gift to Charlene for her baby needed to be accounted for in detail. He squirmed in his seat. Was his whole life for the past few years going to be under the spotlight? He had nothing to hide. Had done nothing wrong, but right now he knew how an accused felon might feel under interrogation. He marshalled his thoughts and answered Sophie, striving to sound reasonable and logical.

"It didn't happen the way the reporter said. I won the bear in a raffle at the Biggest Morning Tea. You, know, the cancer fundraiser that's held every year in May." His audience gave a collective nod.

"I was going in from the carpark to my flat, and I met Charlene sitting on a chair in the foyer. She looked ill, and I asked if she was alright. She said she'd had a fainting spell at work and they'd driven her home. That's when she told me she was having a baby. She said she was excited and looking forward to it. I had no use for the bear I'd won, and it was right there, under my arm while we talked. I was all packed up to leave the next day to come back here to live, so I had the bright idea of giving it to her as a baby gift. People give teddy bears to babies all the time. It didn't mean anything."

His pleading gaze passed from face to face, coming to rest on Sophie's, silently imploring her to believe him.

"That's all very well, saying it was all innocent, and didn't mean anything, Son, but the more you deny the baby is yours, the more people are going to believe the worst. That's just human nature. This is going to lose you votes. Likely the whole damned election." Bill pushed his chair back and stomped over to the window, turning his back on the others.

Turning his back on his son.

On Robert.

That was when Sophie cast aside her last lingering doubts and came out fighting.

For Robert.

He wasn't a good liar, and she was positive he'd told the truth. But his father was right. This parcel of blatant untruths could easily lose him the election. With barely three weeks to go, it needed to be countered; and countered quickly. And very, very carefully if they weren't to make it even worse.

"Oh, bloody Hell!" Bill, still gazing out the kitchen window cursed without apology. "Get rid of that confounded woman, Hazel. The last thing Bob needs is Eddie Patterson sticking her nose into his business."

"Eddie?" Sophie flew across to stand beside him. It was indeed a grim-faced Eddie Patterson tripping up the back steps, yet another rolled-up newspaper clutched in her hand.

"You're wrong, Bill. Eddie is exactly the person we need right now."

Sophie dashed across to the door to let in Oxley Crossing's number one purveyor of local gossip, ignoring Bill's sotto voce grumble about a man no longer being master in his own home.

"You never were. Dear," Hazel tartly informed him. "Home is the woman's domain, and always has been. We just let you men think you're boss for the sake of peace and quiet."

By that time, Eddie was settled in on Robert's other side, demanding to be told the truth, while Hazel regaled her with freshly brewed tea.

"I've known you all your life. I don't believe for one minute you'd treat a woman so badly, Robert dear," she informed him, smiling primly at his surprise. "Did you think I don't know you well enough to discount that trash? Reading between the lines, it looks like Paul Breen clutching at straws. Just tell me what really happened, and I'll be off spreading the word. Time is of the essence, you know, if we're to save your bacon. Electorally speaking."

"You might be able to sway opinion in The Crossing, Ed, but it's only one corner of the electorate." Bill, accustomed to debating council issues with Eddie who was a constant thorn in his side, couldn't resist the opportunity to take her down a peg.

"Oh, Eddie can do better than that, Bill. Just think CWA, Lions Club, Rotary, View Cub etc. Where Eddie isn't a member, she has friends who are. It makes for a huge network of people who know and trust her. That's why Sophie said we need Eddie, isn't it Soph?"

"It is. We're all too close to Rob to have the same credibility. Also, she has more leeway in apportioning blame for leaking the story to the press."

"Speaking of leaking to the press. Eddie, do you think I ought to hit the paper with a libel suit?"

"As long as it can be proven false, go for it, Robert. A simple DNA test will disprove the parentage claim leaving them without a leg to stand on. Now, Sophie, do you know anyone in Tamworth who can get to the bottom of this in a way the voters will believe? There'll be plenty who'll always prefer to believe the worst, but those with a brain in their heads will listen to irrefutable proof."

Sophie stared into space, running through her mental directory until she recalled the sister of her best friend from university.

"I believe I do," she exclaimed, reaching for her phone to call Wendy and ask for her sister's number. "Jennifer Kowalski works for one of Tamworth's biggest law firms," she explained while dialling. "If she'll take us on, she'll have the clout to get to the bottom of it."

"Then I'll leave the proving of Robert's innocence to you."

Eddie, with plenty to go on with herself, hurried of to begin activating her network. Sophie, grabbing Robert by the hand, followed suit.

"C'mon Rob. Like Eddie says, we've got work to do."

9

After leaving an urgent message for Jennifer Kowalski, the next item on the agenda was making an appointment with Robert's lawyer, closely followed by a strongly worded letter to the editor denying the allegation in its entirety and demanding an immediate retraction of the article. With Betty Pascoe's experienced guidance, the true version of the story was simultaneously released across all the social media sites.

While in the middle of composing a mail-drop letter to the voters, which also hinted delicately at foul play on the part of a rival candidate, Betty came to a halt midsentence, annoyingly drumming her fingers on her desk. Frowning, Sophie looked up, catching her eye.

"Help me out here, Soph," Betty demanded, abruptly. "Should we mention the teddy bear? After all, this ridiculous story alleges it is proof positive of dastardly behaviour on Bob's part."

"That damned teddy bear!" Robert exploded, jumping up to pace back and forth.

Sophie didn't need much imagination to visualise a long, striped tail lashing back and forth behind him, and had to suppress a nervous giggle.

"I wish I'd never won it. I never wanted the bloody thing, and I can tell you, if the gift of a teddy is to be considered proof of paternity, sales of the blasted things will nosedive. I advise you ladies to sell any shares you have in bear factories."

Unable to contain the giggle any longer, Sophie burst into laughter, Betty following suit a moment later. Even Robert managed a weak grin in the suddenly lightened atmosphere. Arrested in mid-chuckle, Sophie straightened slowly, giving him a thousand-metre stare.

"Say that again, Rob," she demanded.

Although looking bemused, he complied.

"Did you hear that, Betty? You were asking about the bear a moment ago. How do you think it might work to use Rob's line and make a joke of it all? We'll remind them of who Rob really is and make them think twice before they believe everything they read in the papers."

Betty went back to abstractedly tapping on the desk, turning the idea over in her mind. This time neither of her companions subjected her to censorious glares, instead watching raptly until she gave a decisive little nod, refocusing on them with a ferocious smile.

"Good idea, Soph. And that was a brilliant line you came up with, Bob, even if it was accidental. I know just how to play it." In moments she was head down, typing furiously, redrafting the letter.

Sophie's phone rang, and glancing at the caller ID, she snatched up a notepad and pen, nodding to Robert to join her as she answered.

"Jennifer. Thanks for getting back to me so quickly. I don't know if you remember me, but…"

"I remember you," Jennifer Kowalski cut in. "Wendy told me about your engagement. Congratulations. I've also read today's front page, and I assume it's the reason behind this call?"

"Yes. It's a load of what Mum politely calls codswallop. I'd use stronger language myself. Rob's lawyer warned us not to make personal contact with the woman, but I wondered if maybe you could get to the bottom of things on our behalf. With only three weeks till the election, we need to disprove the story soon as."

"Okay. I don't have a lot of time. Is Robert there? Quicker if I get the info from him than second-hand via you, Sophie."

"Here he is." Sophie handed over the phone, leaning in close to hear both ends of the ensuing conversation, notepad at the ready.

~~~~~

Jennifer Kowalski, bored with drawing up wills and defending clients involved in neighbourhood disputes and traffic offenses, decided to pay a spur-of-the-moment visit to Charlene Larsen. Sophie's little problem at least had the attraction of novelty to recommend it. With luck she'd uncover the truth and save that poor young man's budding career. In which case she might end up with a grateful politician in her back pocket.

Which would not be a bad outcome at all, she observed with a cynically amused twist of her lip.

Drawing up in front of Charlene Larson's tiny Federation cottage in the street behind the hospital, Jennifer had difficulty finding a parking space in the narrow street. Cruising slowly past the house, she studied the gaggle of men and women bearing the distinctive predatory look of reporters on the scent, and their accompanying cameramen, loitering in front of the gate.

More accustomed to meeting their ilk on the steps of the courthouse, she allowed her mouth to curl upward in a wolfish grin. This was going to be fun.

As she stood to one side, pointedly waiting for her least favourite reporter, Marlene Rosenberg, to step aside and let her through the gate, she was rudely jostled by a young woman barrelling head down through the pack. Following her instinct for spotting a weakness in the opposition, Jennifer smartly fell in behind her, casually flashing her card in Marlene's face when the reporter attempted to join the procession. She was standing right behind the stranger who knocked loudly on the door.

"It's me, Char. Tanya. Let me in will ya?"

Yes, Char, let her in, Jennifer urged silently, poised to make her move.

The door opened an inch or two on its security chain, revealing a slice of puffy, tear-stained face topped by messy blonde hair. With the reporters behind them beginning a noisy barrage of shouted questions, Charlene opened the door just wide enough to admit her friend. Right on Tanya's heels, Jennifer grabbed the edge of the door, holding it ajar long enough to effect entry herself.

Having slipped the chain back in place, she turned to face the two young women. Astonished, Charlene and Tanya gave way, staring silently at the intruder. A silence which didn't last long.

"Who are you? Get out of here before we call the police!" Tanya exhorted while her friend continued to stand open mouthed, staring at the well-dressed woman who'd appeared in her front room.

"Jennifer Kowalski. A lawyer," Jennifer handed over her card as she introduced herself. "Is there somewhere else we can talk? I wouldn't put it past some of that lot to sneak in and listen through the door." Suiting actions to her words, she began shepherding the two younger women towards the hallway leading deeper into the house.

"But... But I didn't call a lawyer." Charlene, finding her voice at last mounted a feeble protest.

"You didn't," Jennifer agreed. "A friend of yours suggested maybe you could use my help to fend off the mob on the footpath."

It was only a small fib, she consoled her conscience, and it looked as if the poor, dumb kid could use her help, which would make everything alright in the end.

"They've been knocking on the door and calling out at me for ages. Can you really get rid of them?"

Moping at her face with a shredded tissue, Charlene began to look hopeful.

"I can; as long as you're officially my client."

By then they had arrived in a spotless, old-fashioned kitchen. Unobtrusively taking in her surroundings, Jennifer, growing steadily more comfortable with her unorthodox approach, sat down at the table, waving the other women to chairs across from her. She reached into her briefcase, retrieving a pen, a yellow legal pad which already contained the data Robert had provided earlier, and her office copy of the newspaper causing all the fuss.

"Now, Charlene. Do you agree to let me represent you in this matter?" she gestured towards the paper's front page, facing them from where she had cast it on the table between them. "No charge of course. Your friend will take care of my fee."

"What friend?" Curiosity was lending Charlene confidence.

"She prefers to remain anonymous." Jennifer held the younger woman captive with her eyes. Jennifer's strength of will prevailing, Charlene gave an almost imperceptible nod.

"Right then. Just sign here to give me authority to get rid of the mob." She filled in Charlene's name and the date on a form she always carried in case of need; and passed it across the table for her new client's signature.

"By the way Charlene," she made her question deliberately off-hand, "how much of what's in the paper is the real deal?"

She was startled when Charlene burst into noisy tears.

"It's all lies," she blubbed. "I don't know where they got that wicked story, but I never said any such thing."

Tanya, who hadn't said a word since Jennifer had got Charlene on side, blushed a fiery red, hiding her face in her hands.

Jennifer put two and two together and was pretty sure she had the maths right, but chose to let it pass. For now. Restraint on which she silently congratulated herself a moment later.

"It's all my fault, but I never thought he'd do anything like this. I'm so sorry, Char, but when you told me about Bob Whitman giving you the teddy, I thought it was your way of subtly telling me he was the father."

Now it was Tanya who was sobbing her eyes out, begging her friend's forgiveness in between reiterating her innocent intent. Looking about her, Jennifer spotted a box of tissues and fetched it to the table, placing it equidistant between the girls.

"So." She called the meeting to order, suppressing the inclination to laugh. "Why don't you two make a cuppa while I clear the street. Then we can discuss how to deal with the situation. Make mine black and one."

10

"Right, that's it for me," Betty declared, pushing back from her desk. "My stomach thinks my throat's been cut. I'm off in search of sustenance."

"Is that really the time? Two-thirty already?" Sophie, still helping with damage control, looked at the clock in disbelief. An audible rumble from her abdominal region not only confirmed the accuracy of the clock but reminded her she'd missed breakfast that morning as well as lunch.

"I'll head down to Tan's café and pick up some decent coffee and something to eat for us, Rob. Back soon."

She collected her bag and was heading out the door in Betty's wake when Robert put down his phone.

"Wait up Soph. There's something I need to say while we've got a minute to ourselves." He rose from his chair and crossed to where she stood with her hand on the doorknob.

"Let's go in the kitchen where we can't be seen through the window," he said, clasping her hand to lead the way.

"What's up now, Rob?"

Sophie put her bag on the table and swung to face her fiancé, a frown creasing her brow. She swung straight into the arms reaching to pull her into his embrace.

The kiss that followed was long, deep, passionate and entirely satisfying; to both of them. The only elements needed to make it perfect would have been the privacy and time to take it further.

Knowing those two vital additions were lacking, Robert finally drew back, softening the disappointment of his withdrawal by trailing a row of tiny kisses down the sensitive skin of Sophie's neck, finishing in the sweet hollow at the base of her neck.

"Have I told you today how much I love you, Darling Sophie?" He lifted his head to gaze into the depths of her velvety brown eyes.

"It's not just a line, you know, Soph. I really, really do. I've always loved you, one way or another, my whole life, but until this morning when you weighed in on my side when even my parents doubted me, I didn't entirely realise how very much."

Sophie, her hands still loosely clasped behind his head, pulled him down into another steamy kiss, distracting him from what he was saying.

"I love you too, Robert Darling," she murmured, coming up for air.

"What I was saying, Soph," Robert said, gently setting her at arms-length, determined to say his piece before the next interruption.

"This morning, when you slapped that paper down in front of me, you looked so angry I thought you were about to haul off your ring and sling it in my face as well. The world stopped turning for what felt like eternity, and that's when I realised *you* are the centre of my world, Soph. Without you I have nothing. Am nothing. It was the worst moment of my life, fearing I'd lost you."

He stopped speaking, drawing a shuddering breath into lungs that felt they'd been running on empty for too long.

Realising the importance of this emotional declaration from a man who usually leaned towards the taciturn when speaking of his deepest feelings, Sophie held her tongue, letting him have the floor. His words warmed her to the depths of her being. Aglow with tenderness she contented herself with taking his hands in hers and giving them an encouraging squeeze, smiling mistily at him.

"I wanted to whisk you away somewhere private to convince you it was all scurrilous lies, but with Mum and Dad all over me there wasn't a chance. It wasn't till Eddie arrived I understood you did actually believe me. Not only believed, but you've spent the whole day working to retrieve my reputation and save my campaign. Your trust means more than anything to me, Darling, and I want you to know I'm going to spend the rest of my life proving I'm worthy of it."

Such a heartfelt declaration warranted yet another kiss. Somehow, when Sophie next took notice of her surroundings she was cuddled up on Robert's lap in the small room's only comfortable chair. A position she wholly approved of as it gave her the freedom to indulge in more of the kisses and caresses she couldn't get enough of.

She'd long forgotten her intention to go down the street in search of a late lunch, so it was with a protest muffled by her face being buried in Robert's shirt, that she greeted the shrill summons of her phone. Tempted to ignore it, she reluctantly reached for her bag which had ended up on the floor, and slowly unwound herself from the loose clasp of Robert's arms; a process hurried along by his standing abruptly and putting her back on her feet. She guessed her romantic interlude was over. Kissing her fingertip, she reached over to place it on her fiance's lips as she answered the phone.

A second later, she was glad she hadn't ignored the dratted thing.

~~~~~

After returning to her office, Jennifer rang Sophie with an update on her visit to Charlene.

A visit which was more successful than Sophie could have hoped.

"Here's the deal, Soph," Jennifer said. "You and that bloke of yours keep away from Charlene Larson and leave her to me. You aren't my clients, and if anyone asks, you never were. That way there's no conflict of interests since I've signed on to represent Ms Larsen. I can't be sure how effective it will be from your point of view; but watch the news tonight."

Jennifer, in a thoroughly good mood, chuckled softly.

This case her friend had thrown her way was proving to be infinitely more interesting than the mundane tasks falling to her as the most junior member of her firm. There might even be cause to sue the paper on behalf of her new client.

They really shouldn't have splashed the child's photo across the front page without permission. She couldn't wait to hear what the boss would have to say tomorrow.

"When I arrived on her doorstep this morning," she told Sophie, "it was to find Charlene besieged by reporters circling like sharks who'd caught the smell of blood. I signed on as her lawyer and got rid of them, then persuaded her to talk to me. The poor girl was on the verge of a breakdown. She signed on with me as a pro bono client and gave me the whole story. Correlating that with the information Robert provided on his movements during the critical period, I can assure you he's in the clear."

She brushed aside Sophie's thanks, glad to have finally been able to repay Sophie for getting her sister out of a tight spot when they were students together.

"Got to go. I'm doing a press interview tonight on Charlene's behalf. I promise it'll be interesting viewing."

~~~~~

Sophie spent the rest of the afternoon phoning and emailing Robert's key supporters to be watching, promising them they'd see proof of Robert's innocence if they watched Emilia Hunt's program on television that evening.

She just hoped Jennifer had the goods to back up her promise.

Just before four o'clock, Robert received a call from the television station inviting him to appear following their interview with Ms Larsen and her lawyer. He accepted. This was his opportunity to publicly set the record straight.

After all the hard work his friends had put in on his behalf, he owed it to them to fight back, using every opportunity that fell his way. And didn't television top print in reaching a wider audience?

Putting down the phone, he grinned at Betty and Sophie who had been avidly following his end of the conversation.

"Want to come with me, Soph? I've agreed to be interviewed after they finish with Charlene and your friend, Jennifer. We can go to dinner before heading back to The Crossing."

"Sounds good. I'll just race home and get ready."

11

The theme music was already playing as Hazel and Bill rushed into the main bar of The Victoria Inn where a sizeable group of Robert's local supporters had gathered to watch 'After the News' together on the hotel's super-wide screen.

"Over here, Hazel. Bill." Eddie Patterson waved and pointed to two empty chairs at her table, and they slid into them as the presenter, Emilia Hunt, began her introduction. Impatiently, they sat through two interviews they had absolutely no interest in, before Charlene Larsen was introduced.

"I can't see our Bob getting mixed up with a flashy piece like her," growled Bill Whitman.

"Shush!" hissed his wife. "They're starting."

"And Charlene," Emilia said, "I see you've brought your lawyer, Ms Jennifer Kowalski, with you. Why is that?"

"Well, Emilia, after the way the papers treated me, publishing this rubbish without my approval," Charlene flourished a copy of the offending newspaper with which most viewers were already familiar.

"I don't exactly trust the media." She smiled apologetically at the interviewer, tacitly saying she expected better from her than the papers. *"Jennifer will make sure I don't get stampeded into saying something I shouldn't."*

Emilia stared blandly for a moment, then continued. *"Over the phone this afternoon you said the article in the papers contained a number of untruths. Perhaps you'd like to elaborate?"*

"Let's start with the headline."

Charlene, well coached by Jennifer and revelling in the attention, responded promptly.

"My child's father is not a candidate for office, here or anywhere else."

"Are you saying Mr Robert Whitman, a candidate in the upcoming by-election, is not the father of your child?"

Dot grabbed Hazel's hand. Holding their breaths, they waited for Charlene's answer.

"Absolutely not. We never so much as went on a date together. My take is, someone wanted to smear him and ruin his chances in the election and used me and my baby to do it." Jennifer could be seen reaching for Charlene's hand, giving a tiny admonishing shake of her head; a warning not to make accusations she couldn't substantiate.

"You tell'um, luv," yelled Matt Hendersen, an old codger frequently seen occupying the bench outside the door of The Victoria Inn, schooner glass in hand.

"Told ya it was all bunkum, didn't I?" he muttered to his mate, Tom Carey.

"It could be claimed that you're covering up for Mr Whitman, Charlene. Is there any way you can prove he's not your baby's father?"

"I'll answer this, Charlene." Jennifer leaned forward and the camera zoomed in on her.

"In the expectation proof would be asked for, I've spent the afternoon investigating this issue, Emilia. The baby being full-term, a countback from her date of birth gives a conception date either on or very close to, New Year's Eve. This is also the date Ms Larsen cites as the only time it could possibly have occurred. At that time Ms Larsen was on holiday in Queensland visiting her sister."

"Yes!" Bill Whitman thumped the table, making Dot, whose nerves had been on edge all day, jump and spill a few drops of her drink on the table.

"Quiet, Bill. I don't want to miss this," Eddie whispered.

After a pause to let the viewers take in the facts presented, Jennifer moved on to the next point, ostentatiously checking her notes before speaking.

"My next move was to ascertain Mr Whitman's whereabouts at this crucial time." She looked up, keeping the audience in suspense. "According to his employers, during that summer he had been seconded to their office in Yass from November till the following March, filling a temporary vacancy. Except for two days at Christmas spent with his family in Oxley Crossing, he was in Yass the entire time."

"Bewdy! Told you our boy was innocent, Hazel." Grinning from ear to ear, Bill nudged his wife.

"Shush," Hazel hissed, annoyed at the imputation she had ever doubted the truth.

"Thank you, Jennifer. That does seem quite conclusive, doesn't it?"

"It does, Emilia, but if anyone is still in doubt, the baby's blood group is Group A, and her mother's is Group O. This means the father must be either Group A or AB. Mr Whitman's blood donor card, which he emailed me a copy of, shows his as Group O, therefore we have a second source of proof that the newspaper got it completely wrong."

She sat back, smiling triumphantly.

Emilia went to an ad break, and when she returned, it was to introduce two new guests who had joined Charlene and Jennifer.

"There he is. Sophie too." Dot sat up a little straighter, her hands clasped nervously on the table in front of her.

"She looks nice, doesn't she? I told her to wear that blue dress in case they put her on with Robert. I remember reading blue is a good colour for television."

The "Shush!" emerging from several mouths at once almost drowned Emilia out.

"Robert, with the by-election just three weeks away, this article which Ms Larsen and Ms Kowalski have shown to be an unsubstantiated fabrication, could potentially have scuppered your campaign."

"Yes, it could have, Emilia, which is one reason I'm happy to see it exposed as a pack of lies."

"Ms Larsen suggested earlier, that it might have been planted by one of your rival candidates. Would you care to comment?"

"Emilia, while such a possibility can't be discounted, I prefer to believe it is simply an instance of poor journalism. I've spoken with the editor, who explained that he was on sick leave at the time the paper went to print, leaving an inexperienced junior staff member in charge. This person claims to have been handed the story at the last minute, and carelessly published it without verifying his facts. I imagine he's in enough hot water to teach him a valuable lesson."

"You're adopting a very generous attitude, Robert. However, I do check my facts. Very carefully." Emilia glanced down at the papers in her hand.

"Would it surprise you," she asked, "to learn the person responsible for this disgraceful lack of professional standards is surnamed Breen? He is, in fact, a cousin of your rival, Mr Paul Breen."

Robert stared at Emilia, his rising anger evinced by his whitened lips and flaring nostrils.

Sophie could be seen to reach out and take his hand.

Back in The Victoria Inn the viewers gasped, then held their collective breaths.

"Don't get sucked in, Boy," Bill, who'd experienced his share of political mud-slinging, muttered.

"Emilia…" Robert burst out hotly.

Registering Sophie's admonitory squeeze of his hand, he drew a deep breath, getting his temper under control.

"Emilia," he started again, more moderately, "I'd rather not comment on that if you don't mind. I very much doubt Paul Breen would stoop to such underhand tricks."

"Let's move on then. Robert." Emilia tacitly acknowledged her failure to goad him into foolishly exposing himself.

"The article loosely bases its accusations on this reference to your giving Ms Larsen a teddy bear then running out on her. What is that all about?"

On safer ground, Robert allowed himself a small chuckle. Charlene, also in the camera's eye, clapped her hand over her mouth to stifle her laughter.

"I won the bear in a raffle. Hearing Ms Larsen was expecting I baby I gave it to her. One neighbour to another. As for running out, well... Since there was nothing at all between us, I had nothing to run from. I was, in fact, changing jobs. The timing of my departure was entirely coincidental."

Back in Oxley Crossing, Betty Pascoe was already drafting a letter to the Electoral Commission, demanding an immediate investigation of Paul Breen's possible complicity in libellously smearing an opponent's reputation.

"Bob can take the high ground, Eddie, but I'll see to it Breen cops whatever flak he deserves for this. If it was deliberate, it just might backfire on him."

"Look, Sophie's on," Dot squealed.

"Ms James," Emilia turned her attention towards Sophie. "Sophie. How did you feel on reading the paper this morning?"

Unhurriedly, Sophie released Robert's hand and leaned forward, speaking intimately with her hostess.

"*Naturally, it was a shock. But you know, Emilia, when I read it through, I knew immediately it was a lie. No-one who knows Robert would believe for one minute that he would shirk his responsibilities. Especially if a child was involved.*"

"*Robert, ladies, we're out of time. Thank you for coming in.*" Emilia made her closing comments, and the interview was over.

The crowd gathered at The Victoria Inn relaxed as Emilia Hunt moved on to her last interview of the evening, a fluff piece on the latest teenage dance craze to take the show through to its close. Eddie and Mike Patterson pushed their chairs back and stood, ready to head for home.

"Hang on a minute," Bill stood and waved the barmaid over. "I reckon we deserve a celebratory drink. My shout. If that doesn't cook Breen's goose, nothing will. You can't tell me he didn't know what that weasel of a cousin of his was up to."

"You could be right, Bill." Eddie, more than willing to take advantage of Bill's unaccustomed largesse, resumed her seat, tugging her husband down beside her. "Make mine a port and lemon, please Dear," she said to the hovering barmaid, getting in first with her order, then turning back to the table. "Emilia Hunt certainly went out of her way to be fair to Bob, didn't she?"

12

"Thank God that's over!" Sophie shook out her serviette and spread it over her lap. "I'm starving."

They were lucky their chosen restaurant was still open when they finally escaped from the TV studios. First, they'd both wanted a quick word of thanks with Jennifer, then Charlene had wanted to talk, until a call from her friend Tanya, who was babysitting for her, had had her kissing everyone's cheeks and rushing off.

"That's two of us, then. You Know, Soph, I've seen Emilia Hunt savage some of her interviewees, and I've got to tell you, I was a bit nervous about facing her tonight."

"Me too. But you kept your cool and handled her brilliantly, Rob. Besides, I got the impression she was so annoyed over the breach in journalistic ethics she was more intent on showing up the paper than shredding you. Regardless, it worked out well for us, didn't it? Anyway," she gazed about her as another late couple rose to leave, "we're the only ones left here in the restaurant. Let's eat up and hit the road, so the staff can pack up for the night."

They plied knives and forks with a will, and half an hour later, Robert closed the passenger door behind his fiancée and rounded the car to take his place behind the wheel.

About to put the car in gear, he hesitated, turning in his seat to face Sophie, her face bright with excitement still in the glare of the streetlight.

Impulsively he leaned over to kiss her.

"I love you Sophie Darling. I don't know how I'd have made it through today without your support. Why don't we find a motel for the night instead of heading straight home? Let me show you how much I love you."

Sophie froze in his arms, then gently pulled herself free.

"That's a tempting offer, Rob, but I think not."

"Why not, Soph? From the way you respond to my kisses, I thought you were as eager as me to make love. I thought it was only lack of opportunity holding you back."

Sophie, buckling her seatbelt, briefly glanced his way, her face and body language all expressing a negative reaction to his suggestion.

"No. Not tonight, Rob. Everyone would know what we'd been up to."

"So, what if they did? We're getting married in three weeks. No-one would care. They probably think we're sleeping together anyway. It's the norm, you know."

"Not for me, it isn't. I'd rather wait till the wedding. Besides, I've got a pile of work to catch up on, and it'll take forever if I can't start till the morning's half over."

That was something of an exaggeration, but he'd caught her wrong-footed. Too surprised to think of a better excuse, while knowing the one she offered was woefully inadequate. The truth was too embarrassing. How could she tell him ...? She blushed painfully, glad the darkness covered her burning cheeks.

When she made love to Robert Whitman, she wanted it to be special, not simply shacking up in a motel somewhere because he had the urge and it was convenient.

It was old-fashioned of her, she knew, but her mother had always been so terribly insistent that she wait for marriage, she couldn't face doing the walk of shame in front of her in the morning, irrational as it seemed. Mum would be so disappointed in her. Maybe if she and Robert had had more time to evolve as a couple, she'd have overcome this silly prejudice, but their engagement had been so sudden; so rushed, it had seemed natural to follow her mother's precepts and wait.

Feeling guilty, she glanced sideways, noting Robert's truculent expression. Her heart sank. The more pressured she felt, the stronger her perverse opposition grew. Looking away, she seized on the radio. Reaching forward, she fiddled with the tuner, finally settling for a station playing disco music from the eighties. Music loud enough to discourage conversation.

Slotting the gearstick into 'Drive', Robert cast one last searching look at his obdurate fiancée whose eyes remained turned to the outside darkness when she finished with the radio. The succulent steak he'd just consumed sat heavily in his stomach as he realised she was deliberately avoiding him as far as the limitations imposed by the dimensions of the car allowed.

Tamely driving back to their respective homes in The Crossing was not how he'd imagined tonight would end when he'd impulsively invited Sophie to accompany him. He worried that her rejection of him tonight augured poorly on the prospects of a healthy sex life after marriage. He'd known Sophie forever, but had suddenly been forced to confront reality. In many ways he didn't know her at all. Sophie James was an oh-so-familiar stranger.

Had he made a mistake in rushing into a such a terribly short engagement? He felt he was on a runaway rollercoaster. Out of control and unstoppable, with no idea where he was going.

When his attempt at conversation some time later fell, unanswered, into silence, he looked over at Sophie again. She was slumped in the corner of her seat, sound asleep. Genuine sleep, he wondered cynically, or feigned? Either way, it was obvious they wouldn't be resolving their differences tonight.

~~~~~

"Have we just had our first fight, Rob?"

Robert had drawn the car to a quiet halt in front of Dot's cottage, Sophie rousing from the torpor she had fallen into. Her voice faint and tremulous had him focusing all his attention on her. He took a moment to think before answering.

"Not much of a fight that I can see, Love. I asked, you said 'No', and I respected your choice. I don't understand it, but it was your right to choose."

Sophie hung her head, fiddling unnecessarily with the clasp of her seatbelt.

"You weren't expecting me to say 'No', were you?"

"No, I wasn't. I've been thinking, Darling. It occurred to me we've been in such a rush, fitting everything into such a short timeframe, that we've skipped a few important steps along the way. I thought I knew all there is to know about you, when really, you're a complete mystery to me."

Sophie looked at him, fully, for the first time since they'd stopped. He looked so serious. So worried. Her blood ran cold as she considered his meaning. She'd often heard the expression, but till this moment had never experienced its shivers and horripilation herself. It took a genuine effort to part lips suddenly stiff and cold, but she had to answer him. Avoidance was no longer an option.

"D...Do you want to...to call it off?" She was appalled to hear the tremor in her voice. Tears gathered in her eyes.

"God, no!" The denial exploded from Robert's lips, and Sophie's tense posture relaxed slightly. "Never that, Soph. I love you desperately and want to marry you more than anything else. I was thinking maybe you weren't sure."

"I'm sure. You're right though, we did rush things a bit." Reassured he still loved and wanted her, Sophie was quickly regaining her usual confidence.

"Should we put the wedding off a few months? Or maybe I should give up this election and spend more time with you?"

"No, and no." Sophie was quite definite in rejecting both suggestions. "But, Rob Darling, you were right about those important steps we skipped. I should have explained myself tonight. It's too late to talk now," She had caught a glimpse of her mother peeping through the curtains.

Probably wondering why we haven't come in, she thought, wincing mentally.

"Darling, I'd like to make time to sort it out tomorrow."

"Me too," Rob interrupted.

"Oookay, then. I like to go for a walk before breakfast. We could talk then, if six o'clock isn't too early, then have breakfast together."

"That's a date, Sophie Love." Robert was so relieved he'd have agreed to any suggestion that left his ring securely on her finger. "I'll be on the doorstep at six."

Mutually relieved, they fell into each other's arms. Oblivious to Dot waiting impatiently to discuss the evening's drama, it was a considerable time before Robert walked Sophie up to her door. Declining to come in, he gave her one last kiss and stepped back as she entered.

"See you in the morning, Darling."

"Six o'clock. I'll set the alarm."

13

"So how was it, Sophie? Appearing on television knowing all your friends and hordes of other people as well, were watching you?" Dot, still thrilled with her daughter's success, rattled on without waiting for an answer. "You looked lovely, Dear. So composed. I think I'd have been so nervous I wouldn't have been able to speak, but you didn't sound even the tiniest bit nervous. I've heated milk to make cocoa. Go into the lounge and sit down. I'll just pour it then you can tell me all about it."

Laughing at her mother's torrent of questions and comments, Sophie obediently went to sit down. Idly, she picked up the family photo album, open at the new page featuring her engagement photos. Leafing through the album, reliving the happy days of her life had always been one of her mother's favourite pastimes, one she had obviously been indulging in while waiting for her return.

She shut the album, but when she went to lay it on the table, it slipped from her hands, falling heavily to the floor. An old black and white polaroid snap fell out.

It showed her mother as a young girl, a baby cradled in her arms. Sophie picked it up, casually turning it over to read the name and date pencilled on the back.

"Laura," she read, wondering whose child it was. She'd never seen this photo before. Knew no-one connected to her mother with a daughter called Laura. Calculating age from the date, this baby would now be five years older than herself. She shrugged, opening the cover to slip it back inside as her mother set down the steaming mugs of cocoa.

"What's that, Dear?"

"Just an old baby picture that fell out when I picked the album up. Laura. Who is she Mum? Have I ever met her?"

"Give it to me!" Dot, the colour draining from her cheeks, snatched the snapshot out of Sophie's grasp, clutching it protectively to her chest with both hands. "What were you doing snooping in my album?"

"Wha... Mum!" What was wrong with her mother? Snapping at her and accusing her of snooping, of all things.

"I wasn't snooping, Mum," Sophie protested, flabbergasted by Dot's unnatural reaction. "What's so secret about an old photo, anyway?"

Dot's lips trembled, tears gathering in her eyes. Her cheeks were now flushed a hectic red. Guilt flooded through Sophie, even though she knew she had done nothing to warrant it.

"Mum? What's wrong, Mum?" she asked in as gentle a voice as she could. This was so obviously not about *her*. Her mother wasn't even seeing *her*. Her eyes held the unseeing stare of someone looking back in anguish.

Sophie rose, wrapped her arms around her mother, and led her to the sofa, where she sat, rocking her in her arms and murmuring soothing nothings over the top of her head. Dot sat, stiff and unyielding, the photo still clutched to her chest.

Sophie's mind whirled in dizzying spirals, back through the years; remembering incidents which had puzzled her at the time, but which, child that she was, she had ignored.

Her grandmother, whom she had been secretly afraid of, hissing at Dot that she didn't deserve a good husband after the disgraceful way she'd carried on. This about Dot who had always been obsessively strait-laced. The epitome of a well-behaved woman if ever Sophie had seen one.

Her father, another scary adult in her young life, calling her mother a whore when in a drunken rage; in spite of the fact she never so much as looked sideways at any other man. And still didn't.

Her mother's desperate insistence that she herself not go with a boy before marriage. That she not ruin her life forever with a careless sexual encounter.

Her stomach dropped as suddenly so many disparate memories which had never previously made sense to her, fell into place.

"Mum?" she breathed, almost too afraid to voice what felt like certainty. "Mum, Laura was yours, wasn't she? You had a baby before you married Dad."

Dot wailed loudly in wordless protest and collapsed in her daughter's arms, sobbing. There was nothing pretty about the way she cried.

Great, painfilled sobs were wrenched from the depths of her soul as she poured out her pent-up agony. Appalled at what she'd unleashed, Sophie hung on for dear life, tears of her own streaking her face.

The storm finally eased into wet sniffles and gasping hiccups. Sophie reached with one hand for the box of tissues on the end table, using them to dab at Dot's sodden eyes and cheeks. Gently she wiped away the mucus and held a tissue for her mother to blow her nose, as Dot had done for her many times in the past. When Dot took the wad of fresh tissues from her and finished the job herself, Sophie kissed her on the forehead and sat back, one arm still around her mother's shoulders, offering what comfort she could.

"I love you Mum," she murmured. "I'm sorry I upset you. I won't ask questions if you don't want to talk about her, but sometime when you're ready, I'd love to hear all about my sister."

Dot swung round to face her daughter, horror masking her usually mild features.

"No! No, you mustn't say that. They'll punish you." She looked about wildly, as if seeking the vengeance-wreaking demons.

Sophie, equally horrified, gently turned her mother's face to hers, holding her with her eyes.

"Who?" she whispered, hardly daring to breathe.

"Who will punish me? Grandma? Can't be her; she's dead. So is Grandpa. And Dad. That only leaves Aunt Margaret, and she's won't say anything. Will she, Mum?"

She gave Dot time to recover from her panic and absorb this information, then, seeing her blink several times in rapid succession, Sophie continued.

"No-one will punish us, Mum. No-one at all."

"But... But Da thrashed me and called me a bad girl. He said God would punish me if I told anyone. He said it was a shameful secret and I mustn't tell. He beat me into agreeing to marry your father. Then later your father beat me too. He said I wasn't fit to be a mother and that was why I couldn't give him a son."

"Oh, Mum. That's so not true. They were wrong to beat you. Wrong to say those nasty things to you. You're my mother, and you're the best mother I could ever have. Dad was an evil bully, and so was Grandpa. I'm glad they're both dead." And this revelation of the full extent of their perfidy made her even more glad they were. She wished she'd had the courage to stand up to her father when he was still alive. Maybe if she had, her mother wouldn't be so bloody screwed up now. Anger at how they had abused her gentle mother flooded through her.

She folded both arms round her mother, hugging her tight.

How could I not have known what Mum was suffering? She agonised. *How could she have kept all this pain hidden from me? From everyone?*

It wasn't simply the secret of having had a baby while still little more than a child herself; it was the truly awful fear she had been brainwashed into feeling ever since.

To suddenly discover her mother had been subjected to physical and mental abuse throughout her formative years placed a dreadful burden on Sophie's slim shoulders.

She felt irrationally guilty and wanted to make everything right; but feared making it worse. With her impatient take-charge attitude, would her mother see her as just another bully ordering her about?

"Sophie?" Her mother's softly questioning voice snapped Sophie out of her introspection.

"Darling, do you really believe I'm not such a bad person?"

"Oh Mum, I absolutely do."

Sophie sniffed back tears.

"You're one of the best people I know. Aren't you always first in line to help when someone's in trouble? I remember you being a pillar of strength for Eddie when Stan Turner was dying. And over and over you've helped women in trouble get back on their feet. I've never heard you say a bad word about anyone, not even those who deserve it. If you don't believe me, just ask Eddie Patterson and Hazel Whitman and Barbara Morgan and Rose McGowan. It's not just women you help either. I've often seen you giving those poor Murphy brats a handout so they don't starve when their parents have blown their money on booze."

"It's not the children's fault."

"Of course it's not, although not everyone round town is as generous as you. But the point I'm making, Mum, is that you are a kind, generous and loving person. A good person. I'll bet Reverend Charles would agree too, if he knew the truth."

"You won't tell him! Please, Sophie. Don't tell anyone!" Dot's panic tore at Sophie's heart.

"It's okay, Mum," Sophie used her most soothing tones. "It's your story to tell or keep to yourself. I won't ever betray your confidence. Not to anyone." Although, should she tell Robert? No, she decided. Not even Robert. It was her mother's secret to share, or not share; not hers.

"You know, Mum," she continued a moment later, "I can't help being curious about Laura. She's my sister. What happened to her?"

You stupid idiot! Sophie castigated herself as Dot's tears flowed again.

"Th… They T… took her away!" she sobbed, burying her face into her daughter's chest. "Wh… when they brought me home from the hospital, I went to sleep. When I woke up Laura was gone," she said when her voice steadied.

"All I had left was that photo one of the nurses took. I'd hidden it, or they would have burnt it. All they ever said was that she had gone to a good home."

Dot straightened, putting space between herself and her daughter, her eyes cast down and her hands nervously pleating her skirt.

"I think my Da bought the shop for us so your father would marry me, even though he knew I was what he called 'damaged goods'. After he died I wanted to look for Laura, but I didn't know where to start, and I was too afraid to ask."

"I'll help you search, if you still want to."

Dot's head jerked up, hope flooding her wide open eyes.

"Will you Darling?" A soft rosy colour flooded her pale cheeks.

"I... I have bad dreams sometimes," she confided. "I wake up thinking something awful happened to her and I never knew. I wasn't there to save her. It would mean so much if I knew she was well and happy."

"Then I'll do it." A wide yawn she couldn't hold back almost split Sophie's face in two.

"Oh, you poor dear," her mother fluttered. "It's horribly late, and I've dumped all this on you. You must be exhausted."

"I am tired, and so must you be, Mum."

"I was, but now I feel so happy, knowing you're going to find my little Laura. I think I'm too excited to sleep. Off you go though. I'll just wash these mugs first."

"Oh," Sophie recalled. "Will you set an extra place for breakfast? I've invited Rob to eat with us."

14

The clamour of her alarm woke Sophie from a deep slumber. She turned it off and rolled over to try for another hour of sleep.

Damn!

She suddenly remembered why she'd set the alarm in the first place and rushed to scramble into shorts and T-shirt. She was still yawning when she heard a quiet knock on the front door and raced to open it before Robert woke her mother. She flung the door wide, literally falling into his arms when she stumbled on the doorstep.

"Mmmm… I'm so glad we found each other, darling Rob," she murmured, having taken full advantage of her misstep.

"You and me both. I love you, Sophie James, and nothing is going to change that. We Whitmans mate for life, you know."

Sophie giggled. "Like swans, you mean? Or wolves? I think I'd like to be your she-wolf, Rob."

"Forever, Darling."

Arms around each other's waists, they made their way out to the street and across the park to the track head of the Honeyeater Walk. They walked in silence, savouring the fresh, clean air scented with the perfume of the wildflowers which grew thickly along the creek bank attracting the attention of flocks of the tiny birds the path was named for.

Their singing never failed to lift Sophie's spirits, and she held her head high, drinking in Nature's music and perfume. Putting off any serious discussion for a few more minutes.

Recalling that this thoroughly pleasant walk had been scheduled because Sophie wanted to talk, Robert cast frequent sideways glances at her, wondering at her silence; especially when he noted a frown creasing her forehead. She seemed to be having trouble introducing her intended topic.

"We've got enough to talk about to keep us going for years, Love, but I was under the impression you had something specific you wanted to discuss?"

Sophie slowed, turning towards him. Biting her lip, she nodded.

"We're almost at the top of the bluff," she said, waving her hand at the path climbing the hill in front of them. "Let's wait till we can sit down at the lookout."

Ten minutes later they were seated side by side on top of the pile of granite boulders overlooking the town behind them and the sprawl of farmlands to the south; Morgan's Creek snaking its way across them to where the boundary of the National Park was sharply marked by a contrasting line of heavily treed bushland.

"So, what's up Soph?"

Robert settled himself comfortably beside her, reaching to take her hand in his comforting grip.

"Oh Rob!" Sophie exclaimed softly. "Last night. You took me by surprise. I didn't know what to say. Still don't." She grimaced. Pulling her hands free, she buried her face in them.

Robert once again claimed her restless hands in his, becoming more than a little worried. Sophie was a straight-forward kind of girl. It wasn't like her to get all worked up about things.

"It was no big deal, you know Love," he said, seeking to ease his fiancée's tension. "I don't expect you to always do what I want. You're an independent woman, and I respect that."

"But that's just it, Rob! I did want you last night. I just didn't know how to explain my refusal when you put me on the spot like that. Still don't. So, I'll just blurt it out. I'm still a virgin. You'll be my first, Rob. I know it's ridiculous at my age, but I am. Don't you laugh!" She thumped him on the arm when a relieved chuckle escaped his lips.

"I'm not. He hastily clamped his lips together to prevent another injudicious chuckle escaping. "It's a bit unexpected. A lovely surprise all the same," he added when his love turned on him again, a militant expression clouding her face.

All of a sudden Sophie's sense of humour kicked in and the two of them collapsed, laughing, in each other's arms.

"I'm still amazed a girl as gorgeous as you is still a virgin, though," Rob commented when he stopped laughing. "Weren't you ever tempted?"

"Course I was. Lots of times. The thing is, Rob, Mum did a superb job brainwashing me into saying a chaste 'No'. We talked last night till all hours, about all sorts of stuff."

It took a real effort to resist blurting out her mother's startling news, but she'd given her promise, Sophie reminded herself. She gulped in a breath and continued.

"This subject came up along the way. Seems Mum, and Dad too, were raised in a really strict religious sect. If women stepped out of line they were severely punished, by their fathers, and later by their husbands. I knew Dad used to beat Mum up when he'd had too much to drink, but I hadn't realised there was more to it. I hated him for it, Rob. Really hated him, but he frightened me too. He wasn't above giving me a tanning if I crossed him. I was glad when he died in that accident at the sawmill."

The pugnacious lift to her chin dared him to disapprove. Robert simply nodded. He had heard rumours that Alf James was both a religious bigot and a bully; but had never given the matter much thought.

"Anyway," Sophie continued, "Mum was always so scared of what he'd do to me, she brainwashed me into conforming. To protect me; you know. I obeyed, mainly to save us both from a beating. Because of the way she'd been treated, Mum couldn't let go after he died, and I kept on toeing the line so as not to upset her. It sort of stuck, even after I left home. So now you know."

With that, Sophie leapt to her feet and set off back down the track to town. Robert, a thoughtful expression on his face, followed her.

His protective instincts had him seething at the thought of Sophie and her gentle mother being subjected to such abuse. His own father might grumble and complain, but he'd never laid a finger on his wife, or any of his children. He'd brought his sons up to abhor such behaviour.

Thinking back, he realised Sophie's story explained why such a bright, popular girl had been a been a bit of a loner growing up.

On reaching the bottom of the descent where the path widened, he reached for Sophie's hand, drawing her to a halt. Gazing deeply into her eyes, he made her a solemn vow.

"I'm not a bully like your father, Soph. I promise you'll never have cause to fear me. Ever. I love you, exactly as you are. I'm here to protect you, not force you into a new mould."

Sophie gazed back at him, just as solemnly, then reached up to pat his cheek.

"You think I don't know that, Robert Alexander Whitman? I wouldn't be marrying you if I thought otherwise. And just for the record, I love you as you are, too, and have no wish to change you, either."

The kiss to seal the deal was slow, sweet and very thorough, segueing into hot and passionate. They were brought abruptly back to a sense of their surroundings when Joey Lambert jogged by.

"Get a room, you two!" he yelled rudely.

Robert laughed at Sophie's equally rude gesture towards Joey's retreating back. Swinging their linked hands, they made their way home to breakfast in perfect accord.

"You know, Rob?" Sophie commented as they entered Dot's kitchen. "It's hard to believe that this time yesterday we were all in a tizz over that article in the paper. So much has happened since then it feels as if at least a week has gone by. Do you think we scotched that nasty bit of fake news?"

Robert took his time answering.

"I'd guess most people who caught Emilia's show last night are probably on board, but there'll always be a few who'll use it as an excuse to go around bad-mouthing me. Arthur warned me about this sort of thing, you know. He reckons it goes with the territory if you want a career in politics. And since I do, I guess I just have to grow a thick hide, suck it up and work a bit harder between now and the ninth."

———————————————————

15

Midway through the following week, Betty, perusing the latest opinion poll, commented,

"Looks as if there's been no substantial change in your support, Bob, following that dreadful front page. Between Emilia Hunt and Eddie Patterson, it looks as if the potentially damaging outfall has been contained."

She looked up with a grin, enjoying the relief which flashed across his face. She'd had her doubts about taking on a rookie candidate, but Bob was a quick learner and genuinely sincere about doing good for the country. She could have done a lot worse.

Besides, after working so long for Arthur, politics was in her blood. She couldn't imagine doing any other kind of job. She threw him another titbit, just to bring the smile to his face again.

"I suspect you may even have picked up a few extra votes. Some of the borderline Breen supporters appear to have changed sides."

"Really, Betty?"

Sophie, who had chosen that moment to arrive bearing pastries and coffee, rushed across the room to lean over Betty's shoulder and study the figures for herself.

"Isn't that wonderful, Rob? I've been so worried."

Robert, strolling across to see for himself, slipped an arm around her waist and seized the opportunity to steal a quick kiss.

"Cut it out you two," Betty protested, a smug smile not entirely attributable to the report on her screen twitching at her lips.

"Is one of those coffees you're about to spill down my back for me, Soph?" She edged her chair back and rescued the cardboard tray precariously clutched in Sophie's hand.

Ignoring the interruption, she continued. "Breen's dumped that stupid cousin of his in the poo, claiming he knew nothing at all about it. Didn't go down well in some quarters. Even though it might even have been true." She shrugged, dismissing Paul Breen and his dubious politics.

"He's still your main rival though, Bob, and on the day it could well probably come down to preferences to decide between you." With that, Betty began fastidiously consuming her coffee and Danish, a faraway look on her face indicating she was lost, planning a behind-the-scenes campaign to secure as many valuable preferences as she could for her candidate.

Robert, his arm still wrapped around his fiancée, shook his head in amazement. A real rookie in this electioneering game, without Betty he would have been all at sea.

During the time he'd worked for Arthur Steedman he'd realised it was Betty Pascoe's hard work and attention to detail behind the scenes which made Arthur look so good to the electorate. It gave him a warm feeling, knowing she'd agreed to work for him in same capacity.

Now, seeing her in full electioneering mode, on his behalf, was even more of an eyeopener.

If … When, he amended, *I win my seat, Betty will be top of the list of people I'll be thanking.*

~~~~~

After working steadily through the accounts assigned to her by Amanda Pierce, Sophie was glad to take a day off for the final fitting of her dress. Time was running out, and even though she knew her wedding arrangements were all in place, she couldn't help a superstitious crossing of her fingers against some last-minute calamity.

Once again, Dot, Hazel and Pam were accompanying her to collect their own special outfits, although, from some of the surreptitious whispering she'd observed, there appeared to be another agenda attached to the day.

First stop, though, was to inspect progress on the house she and Robert had commissioned. Hazel and Dot had seen the plans, of course, but this visit allowed them to walk through the display home of their chosen model, and they would also be able to see the colour charts and tiles in situ. Sophie was proud as punch to be showing off her future home and, encouraged by eager questions, couldn't resist rattling on about the furnishings and special features she planned to fill it with.

"But Soph, what'll you do about this house when you and Bob head off to Canberra in a couple of weeks? Assuming he wins, of course."

"Of course he'll win," Hazel, loyal mum that she was, exclaimed loudly.

Agreeing, Sophie wrinkled her nose, then laughed ruefully.

"Maybe we've taken on a bit too much all at once, but we'll still need somewhere to live when Parliament's not sitting. Rob and I talked it over and decided to go ahead. Tony will keep an eye on the progress when we leave. I'll come back to oversee the delivery to the site and the finishing touches if Rob's tied up." Her fingers crossed behind her back, she whispered a silent prayer while answering Pam.

"Either way, we're planning to be in it for Christmas."

She didn't notice the sly grins behind her back, or Pam texting madly on her phone. Neither did she think it odd when Pam and Hazel wandered off by themselves with a promise to meet for lunch. Nobody went all the way to Tamworth without a full to-do list of errands.

Although she did cast a speculative eye over some of the interesting packages filling the back of Pam's car when they all met up again.

"Big shopping day, girls?" she observed mildly, catching a glimpse of interesting looking packages as they drew up alongside her mother's station wagon outside the bridal boutique. Receiving only a murmured 'Mmm' in reply, she let them keep their secrets. It was her bridal shower on Wednesday, followed by the wedding itself on Saturday.

Hardly any time at all to wait to unveil whatever lovely secrets had been hatched among her friends. Excitement fizzed through her veins as she led the way into the showroom.

~~~~~

"Ooh, Soph. You do look lovely. I had my doubts about such a plain, unadorned dress, but it looks perfect on you."

"Of course it looks perfect, Hazel. My girl knows what suits her best. This dress is all about style and fit, don't you see. It's all about the woman wearing it, not the dress itself. There's nothing to detract from Sophie's natural beauty." Dot wiped a tear from her eye as she gazed lovingly at her daughter standing on the dais in her perfect wedding gown, veil and shoes.

"Actually," the saleswoman chipped in in defence of her store, "it's not actually plain at all. Look at the subtle detailing, such as the seed pearls scalloped around the hemline, and the delicate embroidery on the bodice."

"That's right Hazel." Sophie laughed, way too happy to take offence. "There's just no glitter and glitz. This dress doesn't need it." A muffled sob had her stepping off the dais to put her arms around her mother.

"Hey, Dot. Save the tears for the wedding," Hazel laughed, causing Dot to dissolve into full-blown sobs. The saleswoman, accustomed to high emotion, handed over a box of tissues and scurried off to fetch a glass of water.

"Come on, Mum. Give me a hand to get this off," Sophie murmured, leading her mother into the changing room.

"It's not you, Darling. I'm really happy for you," Dot whispered, wiping her eyes.

"It's just ... Just ... When I looked at you, I suddenly thought of all the special moments like this I've missed with ..." Her voice trailed off.

"With Laura?" Sophie whispered back.

Dot nodded.

"I'll find her." Sophie reiterated her promise from the previous week. "I've already begun searching."

There was no time for further private communications as the saleswoman bustled back to help remove Sophie's finery. Shortly after, with Sophie's gown in it's protective wrapping spread out full length over the lowered back seats of the station wagon, they headed for home.

"Don't forget! The bridal shower's on Wednesday night in the CWA hall. Don't be late!" Pam called after them as she and Hazel climbed into the second car and followed them onto the street.

~~~~~

"Bob, you're like a cat on hot bricks. Calm down, for goodness' sake before you blow a gasket!"

Sophie muffled a nervous giggle at Betty's exasperated complaint. She was afraid she was in no better state than Robert. So close to their Super Saturday she couldn't sit still. After sitting in front of her computer half the morning and producing nothing, she'd given up all attempts at work and come to drag her fiancé off to lunch. Seeing how flustered he was this morning, she didn't think he was achieving anything useful either, although she suspected some of his distraction could be down to the aftereffects of the buck's party last night.

As the Lord was her witness, she knew for sure the ladies at her own party had plied her with one or two champagne cocktails more than was good for her.

"Take him away Sophie; and keep him out of my hair for a couple of hours," Betty ordered.

"There's not much more either of us can do till after the weekend. Then we'll busier than ever getting him off to Canberra. Or else we'll both be looking for new jobs." She laughed rather grimly, then added, "If the constituents get a look at him in this mood that just might be on the cards."

Sophie frowned. Everyone she'd been talking to lately had sounded super confident that Robert would be a shoe-in.

"I thought when we came out okay after that episode with Charlene that all the polls were in Rob's favour. Was I wrong, Betty?" She couldn't bear to think she'd been blasé about Rob's chances if he'd needed her support.

"They are, Soph, but elections can be tricky, especially for someone relatively new to the game,' Betty assured her. "I don't believe in tempting fate by counting our votes before they're cast. You two go and have lunch, and don't let my caution get you down. Go on. Off you go." She made shooing gestures at them so they laughingly obeyed.

"Come on, Rob. I want to show you what the girls gave me last night," Sophie said, twining her arm through his as they departed.

~~~~~

Ten minutes later Sophie was waving at the dining table strewn with gifts.

"Up in Tamworth on Monday, I just thought Pam was interested when she asked me loads of questions while we were looking at the house. Seems she had been designated to find out what we already have and what colours we want for our kitchen. All the ladies coming to my bridal shower had chipped in and Pam and Hazel put together all this stuff to kit out our kitchen."

"Looks like they got us everything bar the kitchen sink. Look, Soph. There's even his and hers aprons. Guess that means I'll be expected to take my turn at the stove."

"Course you will." Sophie elbowed him none too gently in the ribs. "It's all small things," she continued, eyes roving over the largesse spread before them. "No big appliances or dinner sets or anything of that kind, but it's all essential equipment. We're really lucky, aren't we Darling? We've got so many wonderful friends."

"Mmm," he agreed, turning her in his arms to claim the kiss he'd been anticipating since they'd arrived. Not much more was said till Dot arrived home for lunch sometime later.

"Break it up, you two," she said briskly, coming to a halt beside her laden dining table. "Sophie, what do you want doing with this lot? Will you be taking it to Canberra with you next week?"

"No Mum. The Steedman's will lease us their unit down there if we want it. Fully furnished including the linen. I thought I'd just pack this lot away for the new house. What do you think, Rob?"

"Sounds reasonable. There'll probably be more to add to this after Saturday."

"Sure to be," Dot agreed. "It can all go in Sophie's room till you want to move it into its permanent home in a few months. Now, are you eating with me?"

"No thanks Mum. We'll grab some food and go for a picnic down by the creek."

This might be one of the last chances they had to snatch a few precious moments alone together before the wedding, and Sophie had no intention of wasting them.

16

On Saturday morning Sophie woke to the sound of rain drumming steadily on the corrugated iron roof of the cottage and pulled the pillow over her head to muffle her scream of protest. The sun had shone relentlessly month after month, so why did the weather have to break today? But maybe it wouldn't last.

I can only hope, she thought, dragging herself from the warm cocoon of her doona and heading for the bathroom, a huge yawn almost cracking her jaw. She should have been well rested; Hazel's pre-wedding family dinner party had wound up quite early, but when Rob walked her home they'd taken the long way. The very long way. And then she'd lain awake for ages, her mind flitting from happy anticipation to troubled what ifs.

Tired, grumpy and thoroughly out of sorts was not the way she'd imagined herself on the morning of her wedding. But there had been all those nebulous worries which had haunted her into chasing sleep round and round to little avail. She'd fallen at last into exhausted oblivion, only to be rudely awakened by the rain.

"Sophie!" her mother squeaked, hand to her chest, as Sophie appeared in the kitchen for breakfast. "What are you doing up this early? You're supposed to be pampering yourself with a lie in." Catching sight of her daughter's less than glowing countenance she rushed across the room to place her hand on Sophie's brow. "What's wrong, Darling? Are you ill? Go back to bed immediately!"

Sophie extricated herself from her mother's shepherding arms. "I'm okay, Mum," she murmured. "Just couldn't sleep. Then the rain woke me," she said, disregarding her illogical self-contradiction. She sat down and reached for the teapot.

Dot sat opposite her, a frown on her face, wondering how best to solve whatever last-minute problem was spoiling what should be her girl's happiest day. Sophie stared sightlessly into the vortex as she stirred sugar into her tea. Lifting her head, she erupted into staccato speech.

"Am I doing the right thing?"

Tricky question. Dot drew in a deep breath while preparing her answer.

"In marrying Robert?"

Sophie nodded.

"Do you doubt yourself as his wife?"

Sophie shook her head, her mouth opening in surprise. Robert had told her so often that she was his perfect mate, it had never occurred to her to doubt herself.

"Has he let you down in any way? Failed to meet your expectations?"

"No. And no."

"Is it being a politician's wife that bothers you?"

"No. I think it's really exciting he's going to be helping to run the country." She surreptitiously crossed her fingers against tempting malicious fate.

"Well …" *Now for the big question.* Dot straightened her spine, steeling herself for the answer.

"Do you love him Sophie? Do you truly love Robert enough to marry him?"

The teaspoon clattered into the saucer as it slipped from Sophie's fingers. She stared incredulously at her mother, then suddenly burst out laughing.

"I'm being a stupid goose, aren't I, Mum? Worrying myself into a frazzle over nothing. Guess it was just an attack of nerves. Never thought that would happen to me." Still chuckling, she sprang up to run round the table and envelop her mother in a smothering embrace. "Thank you, Mother Darling," she whispered.

"I guess that's alright then, Dear." Dot whispered a silent prayer of thanks. "Sit down and I'll make your breakfast. A proper breakfast," she admonished as Sophie went to fetch a tub of yogurt from the fridge. "It's going to be a busy day. Eat while you can so you don't end up feeling queasy later on."

"I'm more likely to feel queasy from being stuffed to the gills." But it was said with a laugh, and she obediently resumed her seat. When one of her mother's light, fluffy omelettes was placed in front of her, she ate it with relish, her grumpy mood completely dissipated.

"Now, off to your room," Dot instructed, whisking her empty plate off to the dishwasher. "I want you lying down with a soothing cloth over those tired eyes. You don't want to look like a hag, do you?"

"No Mum."

~~~~~

At eleven o'clock the James women dashed through the rain to their car and drove to the school hall, the site of the nearest polling station, to cast their votes. Thanks to a small miracle they fluked a parking spot almost in front of the doors and darted inside to join the queue.

"Hi Sophie. Dot. Looking forward to this afternoon."

"Me too," chimed in Angie Wilson who'd arrived on their heels. "Isn't this rain wonderful," she added, a beaming smile lighting up her face. "We'll all remember your wedding for sure, Sophie, since it's the day the drought finally broke. The bureau is forecasting showery weather for the next week."

Sophie answered her with a guilt-tinged smile as others in the queue chipped in enthusiastically with more wet-weather updates. In her grumpy mood this morning she had forgotten what a true blessing the long-awaited rain was to this rural community. In comparison, a few wet spots marring her finery seemed too trivial a cost to bother thinking about.

"Hi everyone," Pam Lanner called out as she practically danced through the door.

"Isn't this rain the most beautiful sight?" Without waiting for an answer, she turned to Sophie. "And how's our bride? Ready to be pampered and beautified?"

"Sure am. Although I'm beginning to wish I hadn't gone ahead with the wedding today, on top of the election," Sophie admitted, a tiny frown creasing her forehead.

"What if something goes wrong and Rob doesn't make it back in time? If this rain keeps up, some of the low-lying spots west of here could flood. I don't know what I'll do if Rob can't get back."

Listening sympathetically to the chorus of reassuring voices, Jon and Megan Armitage, on their way out, slowed and looked at each other. They remembered their own wedding day nerves. Megan gave a small nod, and Jon stepped forward to give Sophie a quick hug.

"Can't have the bride worrying on her special day," he said. "I'll take the tow-truck out a bit later. If there's water over the road it'll take more than these few spits to stop Old Faithful. I'll see Bob and Tony safely home, Sophie."

Sophie beamed her thanks and relaxed.

Shortly after, their votes cast, the ladies of the bridal party trooped into the hairdresser's shaking the rain from their umbrellas. When they left several hours later the rain had slowed to a light drizzle and looked to be moving off to the north. Back home, Sophie made a series of phone calls checking all the arrangements yet again.

Her last call was to Betty Pascoe who sounded confident Robert would gain the votes he needed.

"Since Murray French gave his preferences to us, we're looking good," she said. "I was talking to Bob half an hour ago, Soph," she added.

"He's on schedule and expects to be home this arvo with time to spare."

Relieved of her last niggling concerns, Sophie tucked into the late buffet lunch Dot had ordered in from Tan's Bakery, then she and Pam obediently went to rest until it was time to begin dressing.

Dot smiled to herself as she listened to their giggling 'remember whens'. They sounded like a couple of carefree teens again.

17

Sophie, Pam and Dot, with light robes protecting their fancy new underwear, were sitting down to a last cuppa when Eddie Patterson, arms cradling a box of flowers, arrived

"Yoo-hoo girls," she called breezily, barrelling straight in. "Don't get up, Sophie."

"Eddie!" exclaimed Dot. "I was about to call. The rain didn't ruin our flowers did it?"

"As if I'd let that happen, Dot. Let me give our girl a kiss." She deposited the box and embraced Sophie, careful not to disarrange her hair. Not content with that, she clasped her friend Dot in a one-armed hug while swatting Pam away from the flowers. "In a minute, Pammie," she said with a smile, then embraced her too.

"Tea, Eddie?" Dot reached behind her for another cup.

"Not today, Dear. I'll just unpack these flowers then dash home to get ready. I do hope you like what I've done with them Sophie. My Pierre de Ronsards came on at exactly the right time."

"Ooh, Eddie. They're lovely," Sophie breathed, bending over to sniff at the beautiful white roses flushed with pink.

"You've missed your calling, Eddie. You should have been a professional florist." Added Pam, leaning over her shoulder to admire their bouquets and the chaplets for their hair. Embellished with pearls and satin ribbons, they were works of art.

"Just as long as you're all happy," beamed Eddie. "I'll be off then. I have to stop at Hazel's to drop off her corsage and the men's buttonholes. See you in church."

She picked up the nearly empty flower box and bustled off as an obviously pregnant Angie Morgan arrived with her make-up case to do their faces, staying on to help them into their dresses. By the time she left to rejoin her husband and girls at the church, her father-in-law, Andrew Morgan, who'd volunteered to drive the bride, was pulling up to the door in his stately new, charcoal grey Mercedes. The rain had stopped, and late-afternoon sun shine gleamed on the car's immaculate, ribbon adorned exterior.

"No rush, ladies," he called as he entered. "Plenty of time yet." His phone rang, and he pulled it from his pocket. "Uh-oh," he said, his face losing its happy smile.

Sophie drew in her breath and, hand on her chest, leaned forward trying to overhear what he was hearing. Not that she needed to, as he shared the latest update immediately.

"Put the kettle on, Dot. That was Bill Whitman. Seems the boys aren't home yet. And when they do arrive, they still have to shower and dress. We might as well be comfortable while we wait."

"Nooo. I knew everything was going too smoothly," wailed Sophie. "Did Bill say what the hold-up is? Is the creek flooded?"

"Don't know, Love. Bill didn't say. He was too busy going on about what he would have to say to them when they get in, about cutting things so fine."

"Cutting things fine? They're downright late, that's what they are." Pam snorted. "Forget the kettle, Dot. I put a bottle of bubbly in the fridge earlier and we've been too busy to open it."

Acting on her words, Pam retrieved the bottle of champagne, passing it to Andrew to open while she helped Dot fetch the best crystal flutes from the china cabinet.

"Stop that right now, Sophie!" Pam swatted her friend's hand away from her mouth as she walked past. "He'll be here. A few minutes astray isn't enough to ruin your nails over. Careful of your lipstick," she ordered, handing the nervous bride a flute of champagne. "This'll calm your nerves."

Andrew had barely taken the first sip of the meagre half glass of champagne he'd allowed himself when his phone trilled its catchy signature tune again. The three women lowered their glasses, breathlessly anticipating the latest news. Andrew nodded to himself, a smile breaking out as he listened.

"Righto," he said, slipping the phone back into his coat pocket. "Good news, ladies."

The women relaxed. Dot and Pam even managed broad smiles.

"That was Bill again," Andrew grinned. "The boys are back, and Hazel's chivvying them into the shower with instructions not to dawdle." He put his phone on the table.

"Bill said he'll call back when they leave for the church, so I guess you've got time to finish up the bottle."

"Cheers." Pam bounced to her feet and topped up the glasses. "That'll mellow you, Soph. You're jumpy as a cat in a kennel. What was the holdup, Andrew?"

"Dunno Pammie. He didn't say; and he hung up before I could ask."

~~~~~

"Where are Megan and Jon?" Eddie, frowning, nudged her husband, Mike, in the ribs, looking over her shoulder as she hissed her question.

"They'll be late if they don't hurry up."

Correctly judging the question to be purely rhetorical, Mike merely shrugged. Looking over his shoulder to survey the filled pews behind him. he noted the restless undercurrent. and turning back to the front

"Our crew aren't the only ones running late, Ed," he murmured to his wife, "There's no-one up front yet, either."

At that moment Reverend Michael Charles paced sedately in from the vestry, slipping his phone surreptitiously into a concealed pocket within his robes.

He clasped his hands as if in prayer and waited till he had everyone's attention.

"We're all here to bear witness to a very special, very joyous, event. However, as you can see for yourselves, we're missing the principal participants." He paused, raising his hand to quell the swelling murmurs.

"I'm assured they'll all be here," he continued, a grin spreading over his face. "Eventually. Let's enjoy a little music while we wait." He signalled to Poppy MacIntosh, The Crossing's organist for as long as most of the assembled congregation could remember.

Poppy, never reluctant to perform, jumped at the opportunity to air some of her all-time favourite songs. She pumped enthusiastically, and the aging church organ wheezed out the opening bars of 'Eleanor Rigby'. Reverend Charles, grinning even more broadly, raised his fine baritone to lead his flock in a very non-ecclesiastical sing-along to while away the time.

'Under the Boardwalk' was being belted out at full volume when Megan and Jon Armitage, their young daughter, Chloe, hoisted high in her father's arms, slid into the pew beside Eddie. The song faded to nothing as everyone craned their necks to see what was happening.

"Picked up a puncture on the back road home. Flat spare and no pump. Gave Tony a lecture on basic maintenance and got them going again," Jon cheerfully informed his in-laws, his voice carrying to several neighbouring pews. In clearly audible whispers the news was rapidly passed round the church to everyone else.

Hard on their heels, a harried looking Hazel and Bill Whitman marched down the aisle to join their daughter-in-law and grandchildren in the front pew.

"Bride's pulling up out front," announced Joey Lambert, whose height, and position beside a window gave him the best view.

Reverend Charles, who'd disappeared into the vestry, reappeared, briskly leading the groom and best man to their positions before the altar. Those seated close to the front saw a tiny runnel of water trickling from Tony's slicked-back hair to soak into his collar.

Poppy, once more responding to her cue, segued into the bridal march as Andrew Morgan slid into his pew to join his family.

The rustling and scuffling as everyone tried to be first to catch a glimpse of the bride, stilled when Pam, silken skirts in her favourite deep rose, paced sedately down the short aisle, eyes firmly fixed on the stained-glass window above the altar. As she was heard to say later, after hearing a rousing rendition of the Rolling Stones classic pouring out from the church as they drew up, she'd been afraid of bursting out laughing if she accidently caught anyone's eye.

When Pam reached her place, Sophie, her slim figure, rich brown hair and deceptively simple gown leading people to compare her with Prince Harry's Megan whose wedding they'd all watched so recently on television, stepped through the door on her mother's arm. Dot had argued over that break in tradition, but Sophie had been adamant. "I've got no male relatives I care to acknowledge," she'd said. "I owe everything to you, Mum, and It's you I want by my side."

Robert Whitman, turning to watch his bride make her entry, was held spellbound. The vision that was Sophie James filled him to the exclusion of all else, and when her gentle smile brightened to beaming radiance on catching his eye, he knew he'd never look at another woman as long as he lived. His Sophie held his heart, now and forever.

He reverently took her hand as she stepped into her place at his side, their eyes locked rapturously together. Reverend Charles cleared his throat, and Tony Whitman nudged his brother, breaking his trance and reminding him of where he was.

Happy tears rose to Sophie's eyes, but she blinked them away, her smile continuing to illuminate her face.

"Dearly beloved, we are gathered here today …"

They both made their responses in firm, clear tones, but afterwards, Robert, dazzled throughout by his beautiful bride, would have been hard pressed to recall exactly what he'd said. Although he'd never forget the last lines:

"… I now pronounce you husband and wife. You may kiss the bride."

His enthusiastic compliance with this last command raised a wolf-whistle from the back of the church, and another not-so-gentle nudge from his brother.

18

Robert and Sophie had barely taken their places at the top table when they were abruptly reminded that their wedding wasn't the only important event taking place that Saturday.

Betty Pascoe, whom they'd last seen flinging rice at them back at the church, slipped between their chairs.

"Congratulations you two," she whispered. She knocked her flower garden of a hat askew leaning in to kiss them both on their cheeks.

"Polls are just closing. I'm off to scrutinise the count for your team, Bob, dear. I'll phone when it's time for you to put in an appearance, but no doubt it'll be hours yet, judging by past elections, so you just enjoy the reception."

"But … Aren't you going to stay for the meal?"

"No Sophie. Your mother has arranged for food to be sent across to the hall where the votes will be counted. I'll eat there with the other scrutineers. It was a lovely wedding. Now I'm off to do my duty. Save some cake for me."

Before either one could protest further, she'd kissed them both again and quickstepped out through the door of the auditorium, barely avoiding a collision with the first of the servers bringing in the first course of the wedding breakfast.

"Oh dear, Rob. I feel so guilty," Sophie murmured.

"After all her hard work on our behalf, Betty deserves to stay and enjoy the party. It really was silly of me to try to cram everything in on the same day, wasn't it?"

"But you've pulled it off, Darling. No need to start second-guessing yourself now. Besides, I'm so glad we don't have to wait any longer."

Robert squeezed her hand and tipped her chin up to kiss her lightly on the lips, his body quickening when she blushed.

"Don't worry, Dear." Dot leaned round behind Tony and patted her on the arm.

"Betty already told me she wouldn't be staying. And you know, she lives and breathes politics. A wedding definitely takes second place to an election for our Betty."

"I guess so." Sophie still sounded less than happy with the situation.

"When she calls, I'll round up a few bottles of champagne to take down for the team, and if it's not too late, they can all come back here and party on with this lot."

Robert waved a hand at their guests filling the auditorium.

"I'll bribe the band to stay late."

"Sounds like a plan," Tony chipped in. "Now forget about the election and tuck into this spread." He picked up his knife and fork and suited actions to words.

~~~~~

The phone in Bill Whitman's pocket vibrated wildly, dragging his attention away from his earnest conversation with Andrew Morgan on the prospects for a good harvest now that the drought had finally broken.

"Damn nuisance of a thing," he muttered, pulling it out. "Betty Pascoe," he answered his friend's unspoken question. "Thought it wouldn't look good for the boy to be hanging on his phone during the wedding." Raising it to his ear, he signalled to Hazel to join him.

"We'll be there Betty. Stall 'em till we arrive, will you." He pocketed the phone. "Time to round up the kids and get across the street to the school hall, Hazel. Betty reckons the count will be completed in about half an hour."

~~~~~

It wasn't just the candidate and his brand-new wife who hurried across the street. The Whitman Family went en masse, followed by the majority of the wedding guests, most of whom considered they had a vested interest in the outcome of the election.

"We'll be back. Win or lose, this party isn't over yet," Alan Morgan reminded the club staff.

"You betcha."

"Too right!"

"That's for sure."

A cacophony of voices seconded Alan as the guests, glasses in hands, trailed noisily over to the school hall.

"Up here, Bob. You too, Sophie." Betty Pascoe swooped on her principals and urged them up onto the stage where the chief electoral officer, Rod Stein, was filling in the whiteboard with the results as they were phoned in from each of the polling stations. A running tally down the side revealed that, as expected, Robert and his chief rival, Paul Breen, were running neck and neck. Only the results from Kupara Creek were still to come.

Among the crowd of journalists covering the by-election, Emilia Hunt and Marlene Rosenberg were the most easily recognised.

"Over here, Robert. Sophie. I reckon our viewers will enjoy hearing from a couple brave enough to double up their wedding day with an election."

"More like foolhardy, Emilia," laughed Sophie, picking up her skirts as she stepped forward. "I'm so giddy with excitement I feel I'm about to explode."

When Emilia wound up her short interview, Marlene stepped forward with an extra question or two, at the conclusion of which, she slyly reached into her capacious bag.

"Here's a little present for you, Bob, from everyone on the news desk. We thought you might appreciate it, after all the fuss a few weeks ago."

"A teddy bear!" Nonplussed, Robert automatically accepted the gift Marlene thrust into his arms.

It was dressed in a suit and had one of his campaign badges tied around its neck by a ribbon in his colours. Sophie burst out laughing.

"He's beautiful, Rob. Let's make him your mascot from now on. I'm sure he'll bring you luck."

Rod Stein, a slip of paper in hand, strode into the room, marker to the ready. A sudden silence ensued, everyone turning to face the whiteboard.

"Kupara's just phoned in the last count," he announced, "We've double checked the figures, and have a result."

He began jotting numbers in carefully, eliciting the maximum drama from the situation.

Whispers echoed round the hall as everyone did the arithmetic.

"Hooray!" Betty Pascoe shouted, and danced Robert round on the spot.

"We did it, Bobby! You're in! The Kupara mob have always been loyal to Arthur. Looks like they listened to him and switched their allegiance to you."

She handed him off to Sophie who had no time for more than a congratulatory kiss which was caught by the media cameras, before she was elbowed aside by an avalanche of well-wishers.

Shortly after, Paul Breen stepped up to the microphone to make a short, elegant speech conceding defeat. Then it was Robert's turn to thank his supporters and officially claim the seat. Before he came to an end, a steady stream of people had begun returning to the club to share the news and continue the party.

"Seems there's another shindig on tonight," he concluded, noting his dwindling audience. "Why don't you all come on over to the bowling club and drink a toast to my beautiful wife, without whom I couldn't have won this by-election. Even all you opposition supporters. You're all welcome."

~~~~~

The open invitation was well received, and the party kicked on enthusiastically till the early hours of the morning when the club manager finally called time.

Sophie and Robert, the guests of honour, had slipped away much earlier. With an immediate move to Canberra looming in the next few days, they couldn't afford to waste a minute of their abbreviated honeymoon.

THE END

_____

I hope you enjoyed reading *Electing Robert Whitman*

ELECTING ROBERT WHITMAN

Please turn the page for a preview of Lena West's next Oxley Crossing Romance, *Redeeming Josh Marten*.

Here is Your Preview of

Redeeming Josh Marten

An Oxley Crossing Romance, Book 5 in the series

LENA WEST

1

Thea Benson ran her hands through her hair and took a quick turn around her tiny lounge room to stand, hands on hips, glaring down at the report lying on the coffee table.

"Huh!"

She flung herself back onto the settee, leaned forward and picked up the mug of Russian Caravan tea which was now almost too cold to drink. It was just as well today was a late start, since this bombshell had arrived by courier before she'd finished breakfast.

With her other hand, she picked up the report she was finding so unexpectedly troubling. If she'd ever stopped to think the matter through, which she never had, she would have expected to be over the moon at this successful outcome.

Instead, she discovered this wasn't the end at all. It was the beginning of a whole slew of new considerations. Worrying considerations, she thought, rubbing her temples as she became aware of an incipient headache brewing. What to do?

She could pick up the phone and call the number Alexis Jones, the investigator, had listed and say ... What?

How should she introduce herself?

"Guess what? I'm ..." she tried the words on for size only to find they didn't fit at all well. What if her call brought on a heart attack?

And what if she rejects me outright? Thea cringed inwardly. *How will I handle that?*

This wasn't some feel-good television show where a happy outcome was assured. This thought had occurred to her before, to be hastily brushed aside as irrelevant since there had been nothing to be done until Alexis Jones completed her investigation.

But now the search was completed. Successfully. And she was faced with deciding how to use the information.

Any action of hers was going to impact not only on herself, which could be bad enough, but also on the person who was the unknowing subject of her curiosity.

I have the right to know, she thought.

She did. But at the same time, that other person had an equal right to privacy. A person whose reaction to a face-to-face confrontation she had no way of gauging.

For God's sake, I have no idea how I feel. I'm certainly in no position to make assumptions about their feelings.

All I've got is a name. Just a name. No why.

And the 'why', she suddenly realised was what was at the heart of her inquiries.

At the heart of her need to know The 'why' even more than the 'who' had been.

But what if finding my answers ruins someone else's life? Can I live with knowing I've caused harm to others, however unwitting? Even though they're anonymous strangers?

But they won't be strangers then, she thought a moment later. *I'll have met them by then, and they'll be real to me.*

Draining her now unpleasantly cold mug of tea, she jumped to her feet, tossing the report down again. She was achieving nothing, just recycling the same questions over and over in her mind, and it was time to go to work.

One thing though, she told herself, *I know I won't just go blundering in. Somehow, I have to be certain I won't be causing harm before I act on what I've just learned.*

By the time she parked outside the shopping mall where 'Hair Today' was located, she'd decided on her initial course of action.

~~~~~

Arms akimbo, Josh Marten surveyed the property. The Old Murchison Place, the estate agent had called it. It was pretty rundown, but these old places were built to last, and he had the skills to restore it to its former glory. His eyes glowed as he envisioned the place when he'd finished with it. However, it wasn't just the house he was interested in. The house was the least of the property's attractions.

Close to the essential amenities, but far enough off the main road to guarantee his privacy, this property offered a large, cleared, level space to build his workshop.

And when it came to his workshop, Josh knew precisely what he wanted. A humungous shed, with tons of storage space and room to work on even the biggest pieces commissioned for outdoor venues.

Just yesterday, after he'd found this place, he had signed the contract for a shed which met all his stringent requirements. When he gave them the go-ahead, 'Dinkie-di Aussie Sheds' would have it up on his block in a few weeks.

There were so many new ideas crowding into his mind, he needed to get back to work.

Soon as.

Before his brain exploded.

It had taken a long time to reach the point where he could make a living from his sculptures, but after winning that competition, he'd kicked his day job last week and could now call himself a professional, full-time sculptor.

He turned to share his joy with Ellie, and his face fell, darkness descending.

There was no Ellie. And it was his own damned fault. A man was supposed to protect his woman.

It took a long moment to get his emotions under control, but by then his euphoric mood had evaporated.

Grimly, he glanced up at the neglected Federation farmhouse. The old girl sure needed a makeover. He'd be living in his old caravan for quite a while still, he guessed, but it had been home for so long already, a few more months would be no particular hardship.

Trying vainly to rekindle his earlier enthusiasm, he picked up his toolbox and a notepad and warily picked his way through the waist-high weeds, town-bred eyes open for snakes. He made a mental note to have the yard slashed before he set foot inside the gate again. Meanwhile, he'd go over the house with a fine-toothed comb before he made an offer. Maybe he could chisel a bit off the asking price. Money was going to be tight for the foreseeable future.

~~~~~

Thea cruised slowly towards the bridge leading into the small country town. She noticed an attractive metal sculpture of a farmer, his dogs and sheep atop a stone wall bearing the sign, 'Welcome to Oxley Crossing'. An outlying cottage housed the local hairdresser's salon, 'Hair at The Crossing'. A hairdresser herself, *Stylist,* she grinned, correcting herself, she automatically registered such facts.

The salon's neat, prosperous appearance inclined her to look favourably on the rest of the town, but she'd see. Her holiday had barely begun, so there was no rush. Plenty of time to look around. Meet people.

One person in particular.

A frown flitted across her face. She still wasn't sure she was doing the right thing, only she had had to do *something*. She couldn't not act on the information Alexis Jones had unearthed. She just couldn't.

I'll feel my way, she consoled her conscience. *One very careful step at a time. For now, it's enough to drive around and get my bearings.*

Her wheels rumbled across the timber bridge. Past the hotel, an historic iron-lace fronted building labelled 'The Victoria Inn'. Nice. She'd gone online to book a room there last week before heading north on her touring holiday-with-a-purpose.

Her heart beat a little faster on noticing the newsagents next door. *Later,* she commanded herself, cold feet tiptoeing up her spine. She had begun turning in and corrected her steering. *I'll check it out later.*

On down Bridge Street she drove, confident from her studies of the town website that she'd arrive at the service station and garage. Her faithful little Honda was gasping for a refill.

And so am I, she thought, noting the cheerful little café in the service centre. Breakfast was long forgotten, and dinner a future dream. If the menu didn't stand up to scrutiny she'd go back to the bakery on the corner.

An older lady wearing attention-grabbing purple glasses with a touch of bling, obviously a local, since her own car was the only one out front, was sitting alone at one of the larger tables.

Thea chose a nearby table, close enough to strike up a conversation if an opportunity presented itself. This lady had the look, unmistakeable to an experienced hairdresser, of a person who knew everything going on, and loved to chat. Before she could strike up a conversation, however, a younger woman, baby on her hip, came in.

"Hi Eddie. Take Chloe a minute, will you?" Plonking the baby in the older woman's arms, she fetched a high-chair over, placing it between them. "Hi Dad," she called, waving to the man who'd just put Thea's burger on the grill.

"Jon! Look Chloe. Daddy's here." This last greeting was to a young man who'd walked through the back door from the adjoining garage. The loving smile he bestowed in reply made Thea's insides melt, just watching. Enviously.

If only some decent bloke would look at me that way.

Unfortunately, no such man had yet appeared over her horizon. Feeling she was intruding by taking such overt interest, Thea turned her attention to the burger and chips the waitress slid in front of her. Food consumed, she was about to drain her coffee cup when a chance word from the next table caught her ear.

"I was talking to Dot earlier," said the older woman whom the others had called Eddie. "She said Sophie will be home this weekend. Parliament's still sitting, so Bob can't get away, but their house is ready for delivery on Monday. Sophie will be here to supervise."

Although Thea listened closely, there was no more to be gleaned, so she picked up her bag, ready to leave. Glancing up, she found herself locking eyes with a man leaning negligently against the counter.

Deep, intense brown eyes were trained unwaveringly upon her. Eyes so dark they were almost black. Drilling deep into her very soul.

Or at least that's what it feels like, she told herself, trying to shake of the disturbing sensation. Uncomfortable sensation.

As if the owner of those eyes could read her mind. As if he knew she'd been behaving nefariously.

Defiantly, she tilted her chin, slowly taking in the rest of him. Long nut-brown wavy hair tied back carelessly with a leather thong. Bushy, unkempt beard, a shade darker. Stained, well-worn work clothes sporting numerous scorch marks and an old, fraying three-cornered tear on the shirt sleeve. Boots that had never been introduced to polish in living memory. It all added up to a very scruffily dressed workman.

Someone she'd normally never accord a second glance, regardless of his impertinent stare.

Except ... Those eyes.

They drew her in, more deeply the longer she looked.

Then something stirred in her memory banks; but she couldn't pin it down. She couldn't possibly know him. Could she? With a conscious effort Thea dragged her eyes away and headed for the door, still feeling his gaze boring into her back. It took even more effort not to turn her head for another look.

Time to check in at the hotel.

She wasn't running away. It was merely time to do a little strategizing. She couldn't afford to waste any of the few precious days of her holiday being distracted from her purpose.

~~~~~

Having a few errands in town, Josh had walked across the bridge, then decided to have a burger for lunch. It'd save him cooking for himself later on. He entered Mike's café in his usual quiet, unobtrusive manner, placed his order, and then leaned against the counter casually observing his fellow customers. People watching. Some of his best ideas came from such casual encounters.

Eddie Patterson! Damn! He swore under his breath. *My own fault. Should have looked first.*

Eddie Patterson was vitally interested in everyone who crossed her trail, and highly skilled at winkling out their secrets. She'd been targeting him since his arrival in The Crossing, but Josh wanted none of her kindly attentions. He kept himself to himself; and had no intention of getting involved in the local community, no matter how friendly everyone in Oxley Crossing appeared. He shifted slightly to avoid making eye-contact with her.

And found himself looking at the stranger.

The very attractive stranger.

A few years younger than himself, she had one of those short, tousled hairstyles that looked artfully dishevelled. Tinted very stylishly black with frosted tips.

But it wasn't her hair that grabbed him in the gut. It was her face. He knew he'd never met her before, yet he knew that face. Not well, but he'd seen it recently. The same but different, if that made sense. Faces were part of his stock in trade as an artist, and he itched to record hers.

Not in his usual metal, he thought. Too hard and cold, and he'd swear she was anything but. Wood. He'd use one of the weathered ironbark chunks he'd picked up off the side of the road the other week.

She'd become a wood dryad for his garden. He could see her taking shape in his mind, and stared unblinkingly, committing her features to memory. He was lucky she had sat so still and quiet for so long.

Then she looked up. Looked him in the eye, and he couldn't have torn his gaze away if his life had depended on it. He narrowed his eyes slightly; and adjusted his mental image.

He'd thought her eyes were dark. Chocolatey brown.

Instead, they were golden. The eyes of a tigress. No tame little woodland fairy, this one. She had steel inside her, and he'd make sure it showed.

Just look at the way she's staring me down, he thought, excitement growing.

The mystery woman swung on her heel and pushed the door open. He tracked her through it until he lost sight of her round the corner of the building. A few moments later she drove the smart little red Honda he'd noticed into the street and away.

No longer held in thrall, Josh felt himself relaxing. It wasn't till he was on the way out himself that the oddity of his stranger sprang into his mind.

She was eavesdropping on Eddie Patterson's family, he realised. *I wonder why?*

Try as he might, Josh could think of no reason anyone, least of all a stranger passing through, would find family chatter so totally riveting she would be oblivious to everything going on around her. It annoyed him that the two curious questions continued nagging away in his mind, coming between him and his urge to create.

Where did he know her face from?

Why was she eavesdropping?

To Get

"Redeeming Josh Marten"

as soon as it's released – go to

www.lenawestauthor.com

and make sure you are signed up for news and release notices!

About the Author

Born in tropical North Queensland, Lena loves living close to the sea, although she moved frequently during her early years, living everywhere from large cities to isolated farms. Her most recent home has a deck overlooking the ocean, which is her favourite room in the house, for reading, writing, art, craft or even birdwatching, when the local birds come to visit.

After working as a primary school teacher in both her native Queensland, and later in New South Wales where she met her own romantic hero, she took a very early retirement to travel Australia with him, in a motorhome. This idyllic lifestyle lasted several years, during which time she indulged in the creation of story plots and their settings, culminating in her taking steps to fulfil her lifelong ambition to write.

Storytelling came naturally - she had been making up stories for her own entertainment all her life, but it wasn't until she began traveling that she had time to write down some of her favourites. Now published, *Marrying Alan Morgan*, is the first in a series of rural romances set in the fictional town of Oxley Crossing. It is followed by several more in the series. She also writes standalone contemporary romances and Australian historical romances.

She has an addiction to happily-ever-afters, in both her reading and her own stories, so the romance genre was a natural fit, and the variety of places she has lived have all added to the settings in which she brings love to life.

You can find Lena on Facebook at:

https://www.facebook.com/LenaWestAuthor/

or sign up for her newsletter at :

www.lenawestauthor.com

Other Books by Lena West

Standalone Contemporary Romances

Loving Fenella

https://www.amazon.com/dp/B07B3RLS98/

Contemporary Series

The Wylde Flower Series

Forgotten (Coming soon)